Arden of Fire

Brooke McCatherine

First Edition

NEWMAN SPRINGS PUBLISHING
320 Broad Street
Red Bank, NJ 07701

First originally published by Newman Springs Publishing 2019

ISBN 978-1-64531-414-1 (Paperback)
ISBN 978-1-64531-416-5 (Hardcover)
ISBN 978-1-64531-415-8 (Digital)

Printed in the United States of America

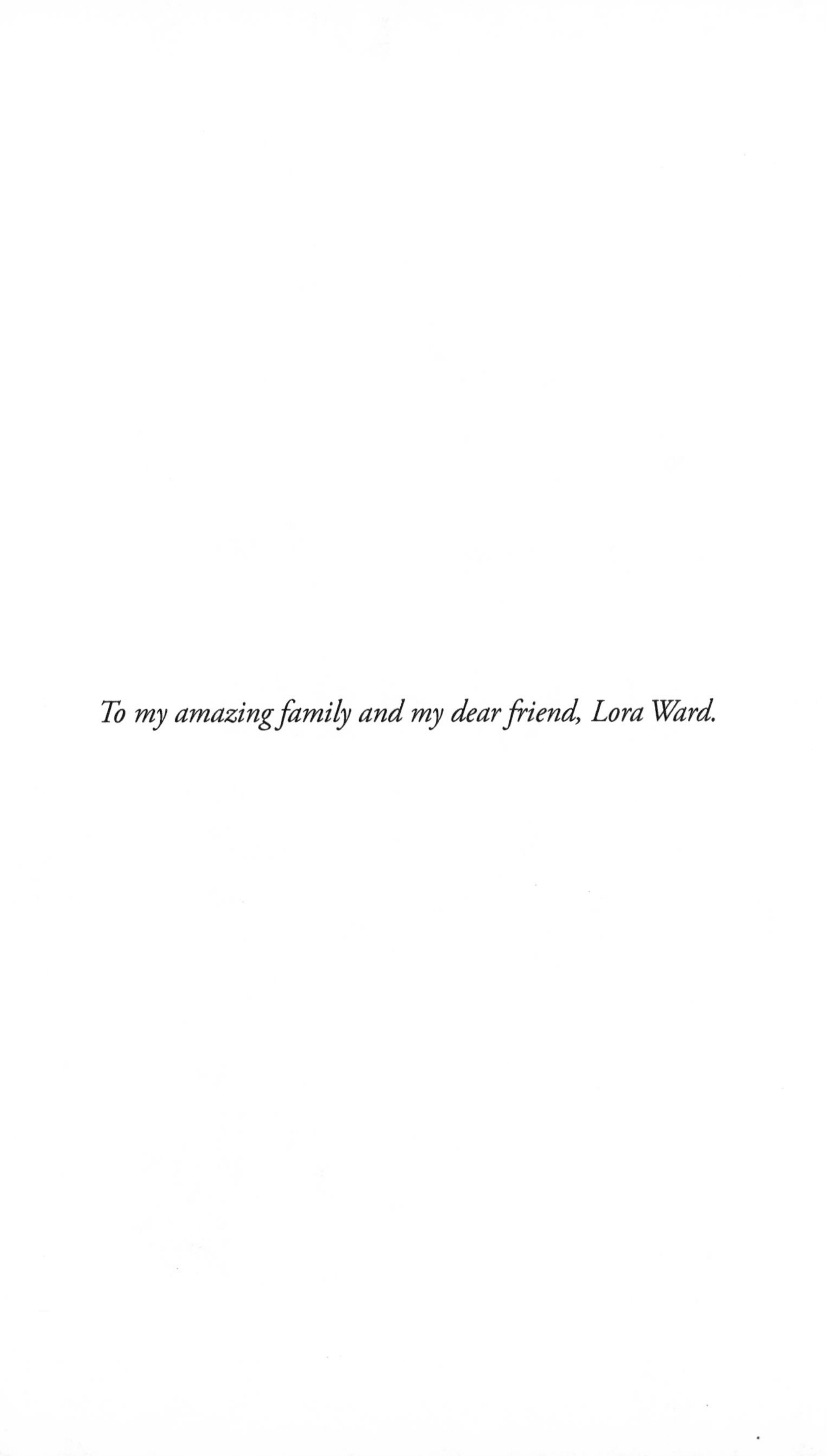

To my amazing family and my dear friend, Lora Ward.

Chapter 1

SHE REMEMBERED THEM. It may have been many years ago, however, Arden sensed her family hovering above and guiding her and her sister, Aspen. Their souls are still somehow connected in this layered universe of observers.

Professor Emory stood in front of the classroom where her words reverberated along the high ceiling. She taught Sky Laws 101. Her voice rumbled with a stern energy, demanding the attention of all students, except Arden. Placing a fist under her pointed chin, Arden tried her hardest to focus, but she found herself deep in thought. She stared up at the ceiling while flicking her feathered pen back and forth. Passionate ramblings surrounded the class about justice and how important The Sky Laws were. A legal system created by the king for his people of The Sky and the humans. Thinking mostly of her murdered family, Arden was five years old when her family died, her elder sister Aspen was only seven. Sometimes she dared to picture what the murderer looked like. What would she say or do to this human if she had the chance?

"Humans!" Arden spoke aloud with venom and continued to roll her blue eyes as if she were all alone.

Miss Emory abruptly closed her book and strolled over to Arden's assigned desk. With a hand on her waist the professor evaluated her disruptive student. "Arden, perhaps you could define Sky Law 109 since you seem to be verbal?"

Uh-oh! Arden straightened her spine and cleared her throat. "*Uh*, yes, Miss Emory, Sky Law 109 is one of my favorite laws. It is a law of good deeds and helpfulness. One that defines helping thy neighbors."

Miss Emory raised her eyebrows. "Good job! Oh, and Miss Kress, have you given any thought to the question I asked you last week?"

"I have thought about it and I do not have an answer for you yet. I'm sorry for the delay. I will let you know soon."

The professor looked down at the floor and stated that time is running out but she understood her dilemma. Arden acknowledged her statement, showing a polite smile with her pale pink lips. She nodded her head in approval before stamping off to the front of the class again. *Whew!* That was a close one. *Hmm*, humans. She's never seen a human in real life but, boy, has she heard about them! Mostly from her uncle, the king. It is said they look different from her people, the Sky Walkers—or as the humans call us, "bird people." Letting out a huge sigh, Arden realized that instead of letting go of the past, she is clinging on to it more as time passes. Whoever said, "time heals all wounds" was full of it, big time.

Tugging at her long brown hair and staring out the large pane window, she heard, "Arden, is your mind in the clouds today or what?" Miss Emory laid down her book with thoughtful eyes that showed a glint of concern as this was not a regular occurrence. Arden was usually focused. Miss Emory made her way closer. She was considered a tall female and radiated knowledge and wealth. She was secure that all who dared challenge her were quickly put into their place, the loser's bracket. "Are you not well?" she pressed.

With a guilty look on her face, Arden responded, "I apologize. May I be excused please?" Without waiting for a response, the blue-feathered girl was out the door and down the hall. This was unlike her to just storm out of the classroom like that. Arden was in a hurry to leave The University. If only she could leave her thoughts behind too.

It was a bright day at Arden's Peak, her home in The Sky, that she was fondly named after, Arden Ivy Kress. Her bare feet strolled to a wooden bench alongside the path.

"What's your deal?" came a familiar voice from behind her. She knew that voice. A strong and humbled voice that had soothed her nerves during the most difficult of days, a voice that carried her through her lowest and highest points in life, her best friend and, in her heart, she considered a brother, Dekker. His warm blue eyes searched her face for a hint.

Arden finally caved and smirked at him. She stood up, grabbing his hand and looked back at the gardens full of flowers in full bloom.

"Some days I don't feel happy, Dekker. Some days I can't stop thinking of the family I lost then my resentment starts to boil like some damned human. I hate them for taking my family away from me." Tears formed in her eyes but didn't drop. She was accustomed to not showing her feelings, a Sky Walker trait. Though the Sky Walkers did have emotions, being poised and in control was their culture. Some blessed Sky Walkers had not experienced much hurt in their lifetime though. Arden did. Time passed between them until the silence had enveloped them to where she could not take it anymore. "I know I sound horrible. I am sorry. You know I am not a negative person. I just cannot help how I feel. They hate us too, you know. There are times that I question King Adao and his ways, but he has to control them as someone needs to."

Dekker turned to Arden and frowned. "Be careful, you are better than this, and do not forget that you are your father's daughter. You are *good*, just do not let your anger consume you as it has Adao. Nothing *good* can come of it."

Arden focused down at her clawed fingers, buying her time to sort her thoughts and feelings. She nodded her head. "I know. In all honesty, I am torn. I yearn to learn more about these beings and their struggles, yet I greatly resent them. It is their fault that their land has fallen. It is their fault their people turned against one another—a cracked dystopian society. I'm intrigued and disgusted all at the same time."

Dekker's posture changed, which was Arden's sign to cease the conversation. Dekker decidedly turned away to head back into The University. She did not blame Dekker though. All Sky Walkers live and breathe The Sky Laws but many have reservations at times.

Heading home was typically the most peaceful part of Arden's day. She didn't live far from The University so she took her time walking the pebbled road, which massaged her bare feet. Even though it was a Sky Walker norm to go shoeless, Arden did wear a pair of sandals at her last birthday when she turned eighteen years old. Her eyes opened wide, realizing that her nineteenth birthday was just around the corner. Time flies.

She let her thoughts float about as if it were made of dandelion seeds. Her dark blue school robe dragged to the ground as she peered out into the distance where the clouds danced with the bright sun. Arden's Peak is a floating majestic island in The Sky. Arden loved everything about this land, much like her father. When Arden's father, Oswin, was the owner of The Sky Throne, he created a plan that ended up killing him. He thought he could meet with the humans and help them, to join the utopian and dystopian for a new world. But Arden's world turned bleak once he and her family were attacked that day on May 8, 2088 in Chillicothe, Ohio (The Nation). When Arden's family died, Adao was rightfully named king per The Sky Laws. There is something that Arden had in common with her uncle regarding the humans. *They belong upon the dirt.*

Arden swiftly reached the long brick lane that led to her home, the castle. She stopped to lean against a tall white pillar that marked the entrance to her courtyard. Her back felt the coldness of the pillar provided as she watched The Sky before her in all its glory. In the distance, she saw the king's warriors flying in The Sky. Their sole purpose is to watch the humans below and make sure there is order and that the humans are following Adao's Sky Laws. The warriors rode on large phoenixes in The Sky, reminding Arden of checkers on a checkerboard.

She turned toward her home. There were many fancy names used to capture its beauty and regalness, but to her it was just home. She was grateful for that sanctuary every single day. Reaching the hall, she half jogged to the grand wooden staircase, which was the fastest route to her room. *Maybe I'll dodge everyone*, she hoped as she hurried on her determined path. Approaching the archway, Arden pressed her taloned fingers upon the wooden door that was made from the famous spinard tree and then entered her chamber.

It was hard for others to call it her "bedroom" because it looked as if an enormous bed was accidentally dropped in an ancient library. A grand library where the greats would devour literature and create stories of their own, a place where imagination ran positively wild. She grabbed one of her favorite books and settled down on her bed, a fortress of feathered pillows and layers of golden covers. Her eyes studied a portrait of Ravel Reed, her favorite writer of all time, which was hanging on cream-colored wall. He was a glorious Sky Walker who wrote of tragically beautiful stories about love, mystery, and The Sky Laws that Arden sometimes wished she were living in one of his books. Many elders did not care for his work for they provoked feelings that they wished to eradicate. What could be better to imagine? She allowed herself to drift off for an afternoon nap as her mind was tired from overthinking.

A knock on the door woke her. She immediately floated to the door to open it. There was King Adao, a tall and muscular man with his semi long dark brown mane tied back with rope. He looked amused. "Hello, Uncle."

Adao took the liberty of entering her chamber and searched the book-piled room. "Did you fall asleep reading again?" A smirk played upon his face that was strong and gentle at the same time. A contradiction, some would say.

"You know me well. It wasn't a 'cloud book' though, just something that I had to do for Miss Emory's class." Arden lied to be spared the lecture. Adao had a history of belittling Arden for reading "cloud books," which was his term for fun books, books that Sky Walkers would read for leisure.

"Happy to hear that," he said, touching his niece's face in a gentle way. "My niece is far too bright and splendid to spend important time on such things. You have a world to help save." He was a natural caregiver even though he never married nor had any children of his own. Aspen knows that her uncle has taken good care of her and she is thankful for that, but no matter how many items are bought or how many endearing words are said, Adao will always be just Adao and never the father she missed. Arden grinned. With that, he graciously nodded his head and exited, saying, "Dinner will be ready any minute."

Arden realized it was early evening. She adjusted her silk robe, exhaled, and walked to the dining room. Arden sat down to a beautiful table setup with fruits, vegetables, and bowls of seeds. The warm wheat rolls were placed in the center of the table and usually stayed there for every meal.

Aspen arrived. She sat down across the table and began filling up her decorative plate. In silence, Aspen's ice-blue eyes observed the room while she tucked her long wavy blonde hair behind her ears. Arden admired her sister's hair, but there was something she yearned for more than anyone could ever imagine—her sister's big red feathers. Like all other Sky Walkers, her elder sister had three large fire-red feathers in the back of her head that ran smoothly down the back and ended just above the arse. Arden was the only one known in history to have blue feathers and she resented it. Now at age twenty, Aspen is finally in the early stages of being courted by a young Sky Walker named Fletcher, an old childhood friend. The relationship eventually developed into something more, love and friendship woven into one.

Finally, Arden filled her plate with blueberry jam rolls and diced fruit and vegetables. Her banana was cut into diamonds, her apples in circles, and the carrots into arrows. The butter was carved in the shape of a big feather. Silence filled the room, as it so often did at dinner. The sound of plates moving and utensils clinking echoed through the high-ceilinged room. Arden noticed that Aspen was wearing her signature emerald green robes. It glowed nicely in the evening light. The colored robes and clothing were assigned as follows: gold and blue were for lawyers or those studying to be lawyers, the green and light gray represented preachers, The Fleet and the phoenix trainers wore red and tan, legal writers wore white and charcoal gray, and law teachers were assigned dark purple and black. Not only were the colors assigned, but each group also had a large letter sewn on the front left breast—*L* for lawyer, *P* for preacher, *F* for The Fleet, *PT* for phoenix trainer, *W* for writer, and *T* for teacher. King Adao wore any color he wanted but he had a letter on his robes too, *C* for creator.

"I am here. I shall proceed with our blessing." Adao came in hastily and sat down with his entourage. He put his taloned fingers together and tilted his head completely back to where his head was resting on the back of his chair and his pointy chin toward The Sky. Everyone followed, awaiting his blessing. "I bless this meal and am thankful for the nutrients that will fill our bodies. The energy is needed, dear Lord, to energize our bodies so we work to the best of our abilities. Help us guide our people, and I ask for your help, dear humbled friend, on my mission to do well. And God said, 'Behold, I have given you every plant yielding seed that is on the face of all the earth and every tree with seed in its fruit. You shall have them for food.' And so we shall, amen."

Everyone chimed in, "Amen."

Like clockwork, after Adao's blessing and prayer was completed, Aspen prays for the conclusion. Sometimes they would rehearse what they would say each day, which seemed a little odd to Arden. Arden felt that what needed to be said should come from the heart and not from rehearsed memory. "King Adao, we praise thee for all that you give unto us. Per Sky Law verse 203, please walk beside our King Adao and enhance our spirit in ways to better understand his words and beautiful doings. Let us walk in a manner of unity, love, and obedience. Thank you, King Adao. Amen."

Again, in perfect harmony, they said, "Amen."

Adao had many men working for him. They would join the family for dinner on a daily basis. It was always the same discussion, how humans were increasingly breaking the laws and how much that displeased the king and his warriors. His lead warrior, Scyth, was always by his side. He was large and intimidating. Scyth was also Fletcher's father, which deepened the connection between the two families. The evening went as expected.

Arden retired for the night. As she laid on her bed, she decided that she would tell Miss Emory "yes" to the question that had been weighing on her mind and soul. Knowing that her uncle would not be happy about this, she did not mention it to him. She decided to go outside of her comfort zone. She played with her feathers until fell sleep so deeply that she thought she would never resurface.

The dim light of morning peeked through her only bedroom window, which nearly took up a whole wall. It welcomed a new day and urged her be the brave person she knew she could be. She was nervous about school today, hoping that she was making the right decision. After a few deep breaths, her erratic heartbeat was back to normal. After showering in her bathing room, then styled her hair with curls pinned up and pieces cascading down. She decided to wear a golden silk robe uniform to school.

The University was as beautiful and grand as Arden's home. It was a white glass building with blue accents and glorious white columns with flags representing all the letters of professions. It stood tall and proud and exuded knowledge and law. It was a safe place and a second home to her, viewed almost as a church and university all in one. A sacred place to worship, study, learn, preach, and write. Arden made her way to Miss Emory's room with her friends, Dekker and Ellery, in tow. Ellery was a newer friend, but a dear one nonetheless. She was the only female Sky Walker that she did not feel judgment from. Ellery was a free spirit who dared to cut her hair a little shorter than the Sky Walker norm. She would wear her assigned robe colors but would make her own tasseled belts to add some individuality. Such a beautiful soul that screamed awkwardness and creativity in a law-enforced world. Arden valued her. Ellery was part of the Ravel Reed's fan club too so they had that in common.

"Are you ready for an experience of a lifetime?" Ellery asked with a body shake to add drama. She clapped her talons to show her excitement. Ellery was looking forward to the adventure they were about to embark on.

"I'm always ready." Dekker mocked Ellery's excitement and shook his body, his feathers bobbing.

All three laughed as they walked to Miss Emory's classroom. Arden took her assigned seat and noticed her leg bobbing up and down. *Relax, Arden Ivy Kress. You are being ridiculous!* She scolded herself privately. Rubbing her pointed nose, she looked up to see Miss Emory standing in front of her desk.

"I see you made your decision. Thrilled to see you here." Miss Emory did not smile but her words were meaningful. She made her way back to the front of the classroom. "Scholars, today will be an adventure. You will feel different emotions on your journey. You will see a different world, a true dystopian society. You have been told how it is on Earth's surface. You have been taught their ways and endured hours of lectures, but now you will *live* it. I have an assignment for you all. First, be a sponge and soak up the diversity. Second. ask yourself why the humans are the way they are. Look for all the differences between humans and Sky Walkers. Lastly, your homework will be to write a poem about your experience today. Describe your feelings and your thoughts. There are no wrong answers here. I want you to know that we will be escorted by some Fleet warriors and, of course, many will be hovering above us. I want you to feel safe. The humans can be dangerous at times, but just know that you are in good hands thanks to King Adao. We owe him everything." She stopped for a second, choked by the emotions in her voice and eyes. She agreed to travel down to see and observe the humans for a day. For those who like the experience and want to learn more, then Adao approved a program that allows Sky Walkers to live in a camp with humans for two weeks. Adao understood that his kind were curious about the beings they control. That was why he finally approved this camp though it was against his real wishes. Besides the camp, no one as allowed to stay on Earth longer than that. The humans would not have the bird people in their environment at all if they could help it. "Now I need you all to stand up and walk down to Mr. Free and he will get you boarded and ready. I will join you shortly."

The Sky Walkers did as they were told as they always did. The group of about seventy-five students were gathered near the plaza where the trained phoenixes were lined up in order. The PTs were standing in front of each phoenix and had complete control of them. About a hundred Fleet warriors stood in a group to the side in utter silence. They took this day trip seriously.

Mr. Free emerged from out of nowhere and stood in front of the enormous birds and group of students. "Today will be the first time you ride a phoenix. A warrior will accompany you on each bird so no fear, my students. I need each of you to find the phoenix they wish to ride today. Let us do this in an orderly way. The warriors will get you down to Earth in one piece. Once you have landed, wait with your assigned warrior. Let's go!" Mr. Free yelled with enthusiasm.

Arden was about to be among those who killed her family and felt resentful again. She walked with confidence and claimed the phoenix whose collar had the name Blaze on it. She glanced to see some others were named Pyre, Flame, Smoke, Spark, Char, Glow, Inferno, and Sear. She liked Blaze. Her assigned warrior was walking up to her in a gallant gait when she realized she knew him. He was incredibly tall and resembled Ravel Reed. She immediately remembered her childhood crush named Ross. Ross had left her class when he was ten years old to pursue the warrior path and join The Fleet. She rarely saw him after this career change.

She cleared her dry throat and greeted him. He acknowledged her and said, "I'll be your guardian for today." He smirked at her. "I remember you, Arden. Do you remember me?" He was good-looking yet seemed humble with his genuine smile and bashful gaze.

"Yes, Ross, I do remember you. You sat in front of me in Energy class when we were younger."

"Indeed, I did. You have changed. *Uh*, in a good way, of course."

"Really? You haven't changed a bit," she joked sarcastically, looking at his oversized muscles.

She noticed him blushing as he ran his hand through his hair. Him, a warrior? Besides the enormous height and brute strength, she would not have believed it because he seemed so normal. He did, however, have the assigned colors and a big *F* on the front of his warrior vest. Arden had always admired The Fleet's uniforms. They did not wear a robe but a warrior's vest that looked rugged and durable. Their pants were made of some tough textured material, which reminded Arden of burlap.

"You are in for an adventure. It's an eye-opener," he said.

"Really? In what ways?"

"You will see. Also, your admiration will grow for Adao too. I watch these humans every day. They are very volatile and dangerous." Ross turned and faced, Arden causing her heart to skip a beat. She looked over at the other students and noticed they were sitting on their birds. Suddenly, his clawed hands were on her waist as he gently and almost effortlessly lifted Arden onto Blaze. He grabbed her right leg and guided it to the other side. This time Arden blushed, pressed her lips together, and realized they were chapped. Ross climbed up skillfully in front of her and sat as if he owned Blaze and the world. Now his warriorlike way showing through. "You will need to hold me tightly. Try to keep your eyes open if you can. It's a beautiful ride."

Arden swallowed hard. She placed her hands around his waist and grabbed a leather handle. She felt giddy. She was about to fly and with a super handsome warrior to boot! *This day just keeps getting better and better*, she decided. Suddenly, they were all starting to take off. She was determined to keep her watery eyes open. She heard Ross say something under his breath, which signified that it was their turn. Blaze's gargantuan wings flapped and create wind. The wings in motion were too beautiful, to see them in action up close was breathtaking. A red wonder. She had never been so proud to say that she was part phoenix as she was now at this very moment. They began soaring like the others. Blaze dipped his nose down for a downward spiral, heading toward the brilliant blue Earth. *This is happening!*

The landing was a little smoother than expected, even though Arden's hair was completely pulled out of her pins by the jolt of the hard ground. She was chilled from the windy ride but exhilarated beyond words. She had never felt so free before! Ross hopped off Blaze and began talking to another warrior, something about the new riding harnesses that the king ordered are said to be ultra durable. Arden sat there in awe and was taken back by the scenery. A deep chest-expanding breath released from her lungs in complete bliss. "This is Earth!" she said to herself.

"Yes, Chillicothe, Ohio, to be exact," Ross commented.

Arden continued to eye the others who were landing behind her and was captivated by funny looking trees. She knew they were trees but they were so green and *different*, not like the large spinard trees that had dark purple bark and bright white leaves. She noticed the temperature was very hot, unlike in The Sky. She saw a pond across the way and realized that it was not clear blue, like their water was. It was a green tinge and looked unappealing. There were humans everywhere, all busy working and ignoring the Sky Walkers as if they see them every day. She supposed that would make sense given her people are always hovering in The Sky above them. She sniffed the thick air. A musky smell of spices and smoke, perhaps. Not like the clean floral scents in The Sky. Arden stayed seated and did as Miss Emory instructed, she absorbed her surroundings and tuned into her feelings. Slowly moving her head from one side to the other for a panoramic view, she could not believe that she was finally on solid ground. She was so distracted that she did not even notice her robe had ridden up her thigh.

Ross lightly placed his hand on her leg and adjusted it in a courteous way. "Here, take my hand," Ross offered and then helped Arden down.

"What is that smell?" she wondered aloud.

"You smell the aroma of breakfast mixed with smoke and pollution, quite honestly." *Hmm, what is pollution?* she wondered.

Ellery appeared out of nowhere and gazed in Ross' direction. "I wanted to see if you were okay, but I can see that you are safe and sound." Her eyebrows bounced. "Now what?"

Miss Emory stepped before them with her back to the humans. "Sky Walkers, you are to not leave your assigned warrior during this trip. Your warrior will know when you should head back. Please enjoy yourself and learn as much as you can. Use your domed armbands for navigation, if needed. You are to meet back at The Landing here in the city called Chillicothe. And remember, do not drink the water. Good day!"

A sense of freedom breezed through them. Ellery held Arden's hand, spotting her best friend Dekker in the distance. They made eye contact. Dekker and his warrior made their way to them.

"Let's get started. I hear that there is a beautiful lake around here, unlike that lovely green oasis you see before us. *Eww!*" He went to continue but was interrupted by Arden.

"Ross, will you take me to where my family was killed, please?" she asked although it sounded more like a demand.

He looked stunned at first but quickly recovered. "We will see that later. For now, let's walk and venture. Let me show you a great place to get drinks. I frequent this place more often than you think. Also, you are able to speak to the humans. They won't bite…well, at least not with me around." He smirked.

Arden walked down a dock called The Landing with Ross, Ellery with her warrior named Ike, and Dekker with his warrior, Red. They moved slowly through a group of humans who were hard at work. A pretty yet peculiar-looking female caught Arden's eye. She realized that humans and Sky Walkers do have a lot of similarities, but also some very distinctive differences. These humans do not have hard hooked noses but also had fuller lips, she noted. The girl seemed to be about Arden's age, but it was hard to tell with all the colors on her eyelids and her raspberry-stained lips. Sky Walkers wore little makeup and mostly golden or nude colors. Arden noticed a not-so-happy look cross the girl's face.

Suddenly, Arden felt something hit her face. Something wet, sticky, and unpleasant. She blinked and immediately wiped it off. The human girl had spat in Arden's face. It happened, it seemed, in slow motion Arden was at loss for words, she did not know what this gesture meant. Only that this human was not happy at all. Ross immediately jumped in front of Arden to ensure her safety.

"I spit on you, Bird Girl. Don't stare at me ever again or my pretty brass knuckles will be in your ugly beaked face." Her black hair bobbed up and down as she moved her head angrily.

Ross piped up and growled in a low tone. "I've seen humans get snatched up for a whole lot less. Maybe you should move on Land Roamer before I whistle for my flying friend." He raised an eyebrow. She backed off immediately then walked away. The term "Land Roamer" was an insult that Ross felt was well deserved. He took a piece of cloth from his leather satchel and softly cleaned the spit off Arden's face. "That was called *spitting*. Humans do that to provoke you. Are you okay?" He looked Arden in the eye. She nodded slowly and wondered if her childhood crush might be catching up to her now too. "Let's get to where we should be going already."

Arden looked up at Ross' face. "And where might that be?"

"You'll see."

Chapter 2

THEY WERE APPROACHING an old rundown building. Arden felt drawn to it almost as if it was a beacon of light in this unfamiliar town. It stood proudly along the cobblestone road, nestled in a residential area with other old brick buildings. Black shudders complimented the black iron fence that surrounded the place. It was creepy but beautiful. A half hanging sign that read "The Hard Road" creaked in the wind. The sunshine hit the place just right. She made a mental picture in her head of this place. It was the first human place she had visited, after all.

Dekker made small talk during their short walk from The Landing. "And then I told Miss Emory that there's more to me than just stealth, brains, and good looks. She rolled her eyes at me but she knew the truth. Obviously, I'm a gifted dancer too." Everyone laughed loudly at his antics as he demonstrated a few moves. Arden wished she could tell stories as well as Dekker.

He was the first to step up on the concrete blocks that served as a porch area that happened to have muddy shoe tracks all over it. Thick trailing vines engulfed the front right side of the building, fully covering the only window. When Dekker opened the door, Arden immediately stepped back from the overwhelming noises that swirled all around. She followed the group and was the last to enter. The air quality made her lungs clench. They made their way to the side of the room where the humans were talking, laughing, and drinking something out of metal cans. It reminded Arden of wine she drank on occasion but smelled much stronger.

"Follow me, stay close." Ross walked up to the centered area where people were ordering drinks. "I need some mead for my friends here."

The young man behind the counter looked Arden up and down and chuckled. "You sure that's wise, sky friend?" The guy responded with a thick accent that Arden was not familiar with.

Ross nodded his head. "I want all dry except two of them. Make those sweet and sparkling." The bartender fellow gave a loud "aye" of acceptance then his hands worked quickly to make the drinks.

Ellery reached for Arden's hand and guided her to a large empty table to sit down. The Hard Road looked rough. Darkness crept in the corners where the walls were gray with graffiti all over them. "WE DON'T RUN" was written in red paint on the back wall along with "THE NATION," which is what their country is currently named. Looking at everyone mingling, she noticed that these people looked really happy. A smile played on Arden's lips as she observed. Music played in the background but nothing that the Sky Walkers were used to. Sky Walker music involved no words, just hums, chirps, and whistles with instruments. This "music" was hard and strong with words, which was somewhat enjoyable as it was different.

"Here, taste this." Ross sat down beside her, and their legs were nearly touching. He handed her a glass that had swirls toward the bottom. The glass was a stark contradiction to its surroundings. It looked like a small beautiful ice sculpture that Arden wanted to keep it forever. The liquid shimmered and bubbled, inviting her to taste it. In a swift move, she tipped the glass back and swallowed heartily, allowing the sweet yet strong fluid fill her mouth. It traveled down her throat, heating her stomach before it dissipated. *Wow!* It was delicious and so very different from anything she had before. Ross looked impressed and surprised. "Easy there!" He laughed.

"May I have another? I'm parched."

He shrugged his shoulders. "Only if you promise not to drink it so quickly. This alcohol is stronger than what we are used to." He got up and made his way back to the bartender.

Even though she was having an interesting time, Arden's nerves were shaking. Ellery was still sipping on her drink and talking to the warriors as if it was an everyday occurrence being in a human place. A melody surrounded them in the barely lit bar. She found herself wanting to sing along and sway her body. The words were powerful, the message strong and alive.

"Who sings this?" The Sky Walkers just shrugged.

Red, Dekker's warrior, said, "It's a very old song called "Wild Things."

It made Arden think about the wild things that she never knew existed. The thought was a little exciting and a little sad. There was nothing in The Sky that made her feel like this.

As her eyes adjusted and refocused, she saw a human sitting in a corner by himself in her peripheral vision. He was somewhat slouched down in his chair, taking long hard gulps from his metal can. She dared to look directly at him. He wiped his mouth with his sleeve. He was wearing a black-hooded shirt with dusty camo pants and boots, peculiar clothing, but he looked more normal than some of the others. Arden would never be able to describe some particular group's post-apocalyptic style. The attire seemed to consist of leather, belts, spikes, touches of bright colors, face masks, chains, big boots, camo, khaki, and face paint. It was all very confusing for someone who wore color-coded robes.

Quickly, his face shifted to the right and his eyes slowly met Arden's. He did not falter or quickly look away. Instead, his intense gaze bore through her. Was there hate behind his eyes? If not, what was it? She was captivated and could not bear to look away from this man. Arden's mouth dropped slightly open when she realized he had big brown eyes. All Sky Walkers' eyes are blue so she had not seen brown eyes before.

"Here you go, you lush." Ross placed the fresh drink from the bar on the table. He sat down beside her and ruined her view.

Darn it! She maneuvered her body in an unnatural way so she could look around his giant cute head. The stranger in the corner had left. Vanished. A loud exhale issued from her as she hit her hand on the table in frustration. This got everyone's attention at the table.

"You okay?" Dekker tried reading her face.

"Of course." She grabbed her drink and downed it again without thinking. *Oops!* This stuff was unbelievable but was making her face hot and she noticed her lips feeling a bit numb. She wondered, "May I have just one more?" Guilt fell over her as she realized she was trying to get him to leave her once more to get full view of the place. *The stranger couldn't be far away, right?* "Please?" She smiled brightly and gave a little wink. She tried to be cute. "Has anyone ever told you that you look a lot like Ravel Reed?"

He chuckled, an amused look crossed his warrior face. "You saying that just tells me no more mead for you." Ross wore a stern look on his face and possible regret for providing the drinks in the first place.

Ellery stood up and announced that she would be right back. Meanwhile, Arden looked around the room in hopes of seeing the stranger. She noticed Ellery talking to the bartender and decided to join her. "He's getting us one more then we will be done, promise." Arden agreed with a nod. "Hey, Mister Drink Maker, do you know who that guy was that sat in the corner over there?"

The bartender thought about it for a second. "Aye, I do. The lad's name is Mythias. Most call him Myth. Some call him Runner Boy. We call him the owner of this bar."

After downing her final drink, Arden's feet were walking out of The Hard Road, but her head was trying to make sense of what Runner Boy meant. *What kind of a nickname was that anyway?* No one in her group knew. Walking back, they came upon some booths set up along the main path near The Landing.

"Miss, please come join me. Come sign up!" yelled a little girl with blonde hair and a black bandana around her neck. She slowly moved her way toward her. A tattered piece of yellow paper was given to Arden. It was the enrollment form for the two-week human camp for Sky Walkers. If anybody wanted to attend the camp, then this was the moment to sign up. The crowd was growing as people were pushing their way through. Ross grabbed Arden by the elbow and guided her back to her friends.

After going through a museum showing the fall of America, they were running out of time in this interesting day. She found out that the humans were rather unusual and resourceful beings and that there used to be "freedom" and a "government" in place. "States" once lived and died however, some humans still use the names out of habit. The humans let greed, power, technology, lust, and hate get the best of them. The day of collapse, ironically, occurred on their Independence Day, once proudly obtained. That day divided their people and a president who allowed this ruin. The president guided the American people into darkness, never to resurface. He was eventually murdered for his shortcomings and for his vile nature. The humans have survived but options are bleak and human rights dissolved. She wished she had seen The Nation when it was the United States of America because it sounded like a magnificent place. A place of opportunity; a place where their people united and helped one another; and a place to be yourself, be creative, be lively, and develop your own path in life. Many occupations were created here, more than just the legal system. That system quickly became stagnant and no longer exists. Arden still harbored a resentment for these people.

The Sky Walkers made their way back to the phoenixes that were lined up as trained. Standing by Blaze, she pet the vibrant bird. Ross seemed distracted and walked up from behind. She could feel his breath near her ear. "*Pssst!*" She turned around, not knowing what to expect. Ross leaned in to whisper in her ear. Warm prickles erupted on her skin in anticipation. "As I promised you earlier, your parents... well, they were murdered here."

Without hesitation, she shot back. "I know they were killed here, but you didn't show me where exactly. You told me you would show me and now I'm out of time."

Ross looked sad. She could not really blame him since she herself had been caught up in her experience and forgot to ask him again. "I am showing you...I mean, they were murdered *here* here, close to where you are standing right now." He looked down at her feet and pointed with his long finger to a landmark.

The breath was stolen from her. She thought her knees might buckle as the world blurred around her. She looked down to see a small marked stone that read:

> *May 8, 2088, Day of Quietus*
> *Oswin Edric Kress*
> *Lynelle Eden Kress*
> *Sawyer Lucretius Kress"*

She felt a little bit of anger rise up, which made her to look around at the humans one last time. Her face hardened, and she felt that glimpse of forgiveness quickly dissipate. She slowly went down on her knees, running her talons upon the dirt next to her sandaled feet. She closed her eyes and began talking to them in her head, telling them how much she missed them and she wanted to know more about them. She did not have many years with them and it was not easy talking to Adao about such things. What was life really like for her mother? How did she speak to adults since the only talk her mother ever exchanged with Arden was about toys, bedtimes, and cloud books. One thing that Arden will never forget and cherish always are the bedtime stories. Her mother Lynelle was beautiful, structured, and brilliant. She knew right from wrong and protected her young with all of her might. Her father was kind, she knew this at a very young age. She adored him and wondered how he lived his day-to-day life as a young boy, as a king, and as a husband. If only the humans were not so afraid of change. If only they were not so violent. If only they would have given him a chance, he would have changed their lives for the good. If only. She whispered a farewell prayer and sent love their way. She stood up stiffly, squared her shoulders, and climbed up on Blaze without the help of her warrior friend. She did not need anybody right now. Silence surrounded her, which was the way she wanted it.

The ride back to Arden's Peak was just as exhilarating. She said good-bye to her friends and walked back home just as rain began to pour. She needed this rain to clear her head, to purify. Arden found herself lying damp on her bed, throwing a pillow up, and then catching it. This went on for a good few minutes. She exhaled loudly, grabbing the crumbled up enrollment sheet that she was given down on Earth. She placed it under her mattress for safekeeping. She did notice the deadline in a couple days. Stupid deadlines! She knew King Adao would be upset if she attended. He only approved such camp for other Sky Walkers, not his niece and not a Kress.

Knock! Knock! She composed herself, expecting King Adao to walk in. But when the door swung open, it was Ellery and Dekker.

"Room service!" Dekker yelled as they came running in with a slew of foods and drinks on silver trays. Arden smiled, her face was full of excitement to see them.

"I was able to persuade the king into letting us eat dinner in your room tonight. Oh, Arden, he is so lovely. He said yes without hesitation." Ellery smiled and had a dreamy look in her eyes.

This made Arden roll hers. "Sounds much more fun than the normal stuffy dinners with him and the crew." She grabbed a handful of seeds and shoved them in her mouth.

"You are lucky. Please remember that your uncle is the king, for crying out loud! And your sister...well, she's doing really well in her division." Ellery said in a blatantly envious tone.

They made small talk and discussed their day trip until nightfall. They laughed about Ross and Arden flirting, which she heavily denied. They really liked The Hard Road and the people there. Ellery mentioned the "spitter" and acted out what she would have done to her, pretending to scratch her face and then run off into the other direction. They giggled and finished eating their dinner. "It's past curfew. Let's sneak outside and look at the stars." They jumped up in unison and headed for the door.

"*Shhh!*" Dekker opened the door and looked both ways. The coast was clear. He scuttled down the hall, leaving the girls to fend for themselves.

The house was like a maze and had beautiful nest twigs stuck to the white marble walls. The halls had beautiful carvings of phoenixes on the spinard doors. A house fit for a king. They ran out the back door and reached a huge garden upon acres of land. Flowers danced in the night breeze and The Sky was a royal shade of blue. Arden grabbed her friend's hands and they ran further into the garden where the tree swings swayed and the moonlight danced glistening across a pond of cool water. There were also tree houses that looked like huge nests atop the trees, close to twenty of them spread across the land. They chose the closest tree and climbed up the wooden ladder to the fluffy nest on top. They laid their backs on the heap of feathers and watched the stars. The stars were scattered and shined brightly as if they knew they had an audience. Constellations twinkled. They made her heart thump in joy. These moments are what made her life worth living. She closed her eyes and absorbed the happiness in the beautiful darkness.

Arden opened her eyes. She must had fallen asleep. It was still dark as she stretched her arms above her head and looked down to the ground below. Large ripples came from the pond below as if someone had just jumped in. *Maybe something fell into it?* She heard water splashing below. Her heart paused. *Is it King Adao taking a late night swim?* That did not make sense though. His entourage would be near and Arden could not see anyone else around. She moved to the other side of the nest for a better view. A person came abruptly up to the surface. He swam around in the clear water. *Who in the hell is in her backyard?* She slid down the ladder and jumped off, skipping the last few steps. She bent down and peeked to get another look at him. This person had short hair so it could not have been Adao. Adao always tied his hair in a ponytail with rope. "You! What do you think you are doing?" Arden stepped out of the shadows and used a demanding voice.

The man froze and kept his back to her. "Go away," he said in a low tone.

She tried to make her way around the pond because the man would not face her. "Who are you? I demand to know! You are trespassing on the king's grounds, which is a very poor choice on your part." He kept his back to her. "I'm not telling you again! I will scream for help if you do not leave." The man walked a few steps, the waterline going lower on his body. He had muscles of steel and strange markings on his back and arms, something Arden had never seen before. He was beautiful though. Then she noticed his hand coming up to push back his hair. It was a human hand. *How is this possible? How is a human in The Sky?* "I saw you today! I know you saw me." He paused. Arden sat down on the ground, e trying to figure this puzzle out. *How is the stranger here?* "You do not belong on the Earth. Earth is full of hard truth, hurt, and disappointment." As he looked over his shoulder in a fluid manner, she could see part of his face. His brown eyes sparkled. Suddenly, she saw his reflection in the pond. Arden was breathing heavily. "How…how are you here?"

Without warning, the stranger went underwater. Ripples spread around him. Arden jumped back, waiting for him to resurface. A minute passed. "How long can humans hold their breath?" She asked aloud. She grew impatient and worried at the same time. She did not know what else to do so she made her way to where he stood. She took a big breath and dove into the water. She felt nothing. *Where did he go? Please no! I want to know him, I have to know him!* She came up for air and looked around for him. Nothing. Out of nowhere, his hands grabbed her waist. They both sank underwater once again.

*****

A loud exaggerated gasp for air came from Arden as she awoke from her very real dream. She looked around and her friends were sleeping next to her in the nest. She looked over the side and did not see anything. No signs of the stranger. Disappointment engulfed her body down to her soul. *How could something so real be only a dream?* Those eyes will be forever ingrained into her mind.

"Arden!" someone yelled from below, causing her to jump. It was Aspen in her nightclothes.

"Why don't you come up?"

Aspen crossed her arms and pondered the invitation. She climbed up and sat down next to Arden in silence. Her eyes looked around the treetops. She seemed to be in a tranquil state. The elder sister laughed slightly. "I was going to ask you why you are sleeping up here but it's actually quite peaceful." She felt the breeze on her cheeks.

They stayed up late, talking about memories from their childhood. The two siblings were close but both needed space and found their own paths when it came to justice and The Sky Laws. A night with her sister was just what she needed to feel whole again. Arden loved to see Aspen let down her guard and be a normal girl. They had an imperfect sisterly bond that would be cherished always for Aspen was her only real family. They cuddled up next to each other and went fast asleep.

Breakfast was being served in the main dining room. Loki, the main cook, came out with healthy foods for the group to feast on. She cooked on the side but was truly a legal writer and wore the assigned robe. Arden grabbed a piece of toast and began singing the song that she heard at The Hard Road. Loki looked perplexed. "What are you singing?" Arden realized what she was doing.

"She's singing a human song, that is what she is singing." King Adao's voice echoed from behind Arden's seat. She froze and cleared her throat. King Adao sat down at the head of the table. His hands were clasped together and he had a placid expression. He then smiled. "At ease, Arden. I know about your trip yesterday and I am interested. I want to hear all about it."

Arden didn't understand his politeness. Why must he know *everything*? "It was different." She stopped to take a drink of water, hoping that would suffice.

Adao made his plate but kept his eyes pierced on her. "And…?" he urged.

"Well, what do you want to know exactly?"

"Tell me what you did. I'm excited to hear about it."

She could not help but to call him on this passive-aggressive behavior. "Really? Why would you be excited? You loath them. I am surprised you are not angry with me for not informing you. I'm also surprised that I'm not imprisoned for days on end, much like the time I wore the wrong colored robe."

This made him chuckle, his entourage joined in. "Sweet, sweet Arden. I sometimes wonder if you not know me at all. Perhaps we do not spend enough time together, which I am sure is my fault. I encourage my people to learn and experience Earth. I approved this field trip long ago. Just because I do not agree with their ways does not mean that I cannot see beauty down there. You say that I surprise you, however, I feel it's the other way around, Daughter."

This stumped her, and she felt guilty. "I apologize. I just assumed you would not like it. I went to the museum and learned about the fall of America and met some humans." She paused. "I was shown where *they* were killed." She took another gulp and waited for a response.

He looked down at his plate. "Really? Well, God bless Oswin, Lynelle, and baby Sawyer. I miss them every single day," he said with emotion. "I don't know if anyone understands my grief. It is not an easy position to be in when your only brother, who happened to be a great king, has been murdered. The grief is not easy to swallow down, nor is it easy to follow such profound footsteps. Your father and

I did not agree on everything, Arden, but we loved and, most importantly, respected one another. I had to muster as much bravery and strength to right what was wrong, hence the new edition of The Sky Laws. The humans cannot be trusted, but I do not loath them, as you say. I resent them. Now let's eat." King Adao said grace before eating his meal.

"May I ask you a question?" Arden asked. He nodded slightly. "If you were tolerable with the visit yesterday, then how would you feel about me going there for the two-week camp?"

King Adao took a breath. "If that is what you wish, then please go. I also approved this camp for those who feel they do not have enough answers. I warn you though, you are not to return to Earth after this camp. It is forbidden, even for you. I have tolerance, but that is my limit." He looked down at his bare feet. "I'm just taken back that you would want to be around their kind for that long, Daughter."

Boy, did he make a point! Most importantly, why does he have to call her daughter all the time? He never calls Aspen his daughter. He must view her more of an equal since she acts like a ninety-year-old! "You make a good point. I have not an answer. I hope I have not offended you, Uncle." She will never call him father. He got up from the dinner table and kissed the top of her head. This told her that she can do as she pleases. "One last thought, have you ever thought of building a large landmark in honor of King Oswin down on Earth? Perhaps a statue instead of the small stone?" His eyes were dark and unreadable. Maybe she has asked too many questions, but it was not every day that she could communicate like this with him.

"What makes you think the humans would want to see such a sight every day?" He paused then continued, "I will think on it." He walked down the hall with Aspen quickly following suit.

Chapter 3

LATER THAT EVENING…

"Got you!" Arden found the camp paper she secretly stashed under her mattress. Looking down at the crumbled up yellow parchment, she was hesitant on signing it. She thought of Ross. Lying back on her bed, she realized she will see him at the Flying Festival tomorrow and could talk to him about turning it in for her. She decided she will go.

The Flying Festival is considered a holiday. Arden knew she needed to prepare for this grand event because everyone is attending. Besides, it is the only day where cheers and jeers are allowed. It is also a day of competitions and athletics. Her almond-shaped eyes closed for a moment, reminiscing of her younger days at their stadium called The Perch. She remembered rooting for her favorite warrior group with such enthusiasm. Her then childlike eyes would widen as she watched her warriors, riding on firebirds, hit their targets with bright burning fire. They were the champions and all the losers were shipped off to a training camp as punishment. Arden remembered telling her father that one day she was going to be a great warrior and win the festival. Oswin's chuckles echoed through her forlorn mind and ears. A small smile came upon her mouth as she thought of him.

*****

At the day of the Flying Festival, Arden woke up and knew she would need to dress fancy for this all-day event. It was a holiday, after all, and all the women would be dressed in elegant robes. This was the only time that the robes did not have to be identical, though the color and letter had to be the same. She skimmed through her closet to get a good look at her options. She even called Loki to assist with fixing her hair since she was good with her hands. Loki decided to try something completely new where she took pieces of hair and weaved it to look like chains hanging throughout her long straight hair. Loki got the idea when she cut up pie dough one day. Arden's eye makeup was dark and smoky blue, which was not their norm but was allowed for special occasions such as this. It complimented her high cheekbones and pale pink lips perfectly. Arden slipped into her golden silk robe that had dark blue lace intricately placed on her shoulders and trimmed her bosom area. The flowing robe was made of the best materials in The Sky. She decided to go barefoot today as many Sky Walkers do, however she did place some gold chains on her ankles. She was ready for this day.

When they arrived at The Perch, it was bustling with activity. Arden reserved royal seats that she shared with her close friends and family. Sparkling water fizzed in the natural light and tickled Arden's nose as she sipped. They chatted over some legal matters when she finally seen Ross from afar. Waving her hand in the air, she got his attention. He was dressed more warriorlike than ever.

"Hi, Lush. *Wow*, you look nice!" He beamed at her.

"Thank you. Have you been practicing for this? I'd hate to see you lose and be gone for training for five months."

Ross seemed somewhat worried. "I have been practicing with Blaze, but it's hard to say."

Arden grabbed his hand and placed the camp slip into it. "I need a favor. I do not want Adao knowing this… please." Ross' eyebrows arched as she continued, "I was wondering if you could turn this paper in for me. The deadline is tomorrow."

"Yes, I will help you. Just give it to me after the festival. I do not want to lose it."

Arden nodded. She wished him luck and gave him a hug. He walked away and disappeared behind a building. She joined her friends just as the announcements sounded above. The A Team came walking out to the field with their firebirds. They were a very experienced and mature group. Most had long white hair in ponytails. Music played in the background. They waved to the crowd of people, which caused screams and whistles. The A Team were the reigning champions from the last festival. They were introduced one by one before they jumped on their birds and took off in a synchronized manner. They knew what they were doing. Professionals. The next group, B Team, included Ross. They did the same. There were so many groups that Arden lost count.

It was an eventful day. They ate, talked, and watched them practice. But as the early evening was approaching, it was getting down to the nitty-gritty. Adrenaline and sweat was in the air, the Sky Walkers were invested. The B Team was on the prowl and ready to show off their skills. They lined up one after another. Red bird behind red bird were waiting for the loud siren to sound. As soon as the siren screeched, they were off. Swooping, ducking, soaring, and flapping, they were beautifully swift and accurate. One hit after another, fire swept over the human targets, engulfing them in smoke billowing high in The Sky.

Ross and Blaze were such a great team! Arden looked away for one second and, unexpectedly, the warrior behind Ross seemed to have lost his grip on his saddled bird. He went out of line and lost total control of his phoenix. Something bad was about to happen. *WHAM!* They slammed into Ross and Blaze with great force that knocked them off. The world went silent as both fell fast. Arden could not breathe. Ross was in grave danger and she could not do anything about it. The world slowed as she screamed aloud. Ross was plummeting and very close to hitting the ground when a different bird swept down under him and broke his fall. They landed in a tumble and Ross was thrown into the stands. Arden was shaking violently as she tried to run to him. People were everywhere so she broke into a sprint. There was not even a doctor around because Sky Walkers no longer practice medicine. If someone was injured, they just stayed in bed until they healed or wait for death. Many Sky Walkers had deformities due to improper healing because Adao will not approve of "witch doctors" in his land. He made past doctors find a legal profession instead. King Adao had his reasons. There was no one to mend Ross, this scared her the most. When she finally reached him, his body was still on the ground. Sky Walkers were surrounding him, trying to pick him up.

"Ross, are you okay?" She grabbed his face and looked into his eyes. He was not dead. The warrior was limp and did not speak, but there was a pulse. She took his hand and tried to get him to speak. "Look at me, you are bleeding. I am going to wrap your vest around your leg to stop the bleeding. Please take some deep breaths. Speak to me." She extended her arm to fellow Sky Walkers and they backed away to give her space.

He was blinking but seemed stunned. He made a small noise when she was wrapping up his leg. Arden was moving his arms and noticed some of his talons had been ripped off his fingers and were bleeding. She then applied pressure with her robe. "Thank you," he mustered.

"You are going to be okay, I promise." Arden asked if he could move his other leg and he did.

After thorough assessment, it was safe to say that Ross had a broken leg, a broken arm, some bruises, and deep cuts, but all were mendable. Ross was put on a cot and pushed into the training building. Arden stood up with blood all over her robe and on her face. She was breathing heavily but had hope that he would heal. Ross would be okay. All at once, she remembered hearing that the humans had doctors down below. She had to find Adao and plead that he bring a medical doctor up to the Arden's Peak. She was on a mission. She searched the crowds for her uncle but could not find him. She ran back to her table to a very worried Ellery and Dekker. Aspen had disappeared. "Where is she?" ahe yelled. Arden knew that wherever Aspen was, the king wasn't far away.

"She left with King Adao toward the training building to see Ross."

Arden took off running as fast as her bare feet would allow her. She came upon the entrance f the building. There were people everywhere. She jumped on her tippy-toes to get a better view. Adao talking to Ross. Arden ran up behind them and heard Adao speaking in a low tone into Ross' ear.

"You are a disgrace to Sky Walkers' warriors. You could have corrected that hit. You were on the best phoenix in the land, yet you still fell like a weak warrior." Ross gave no argument, he was in too much pain. "You are disqualified from the game. You and your B Team will be gone tomorrow morning for training. You need it, warrior. I am sorry that you are in pain but not sorry that you are about to learn a very important lesson." King Adao placed pressure upon Ross' broken leg as he stood up proudly, making Ross yell out in pain. King Adao instructed his entourage to remove everyone from the building.

Arden stood like a statue in horror and bewilderment. She could not believe she witnessed such cruelty from him. She was shocked. *How dare he say such things?* She gritted her teeth and tapped the king on the shoulder. He turned around. She wanted to yell at him and stick up for Ross, but once their eyes met, it did not feel right. Not now. He was her king and yelling at him would not help Ross at all. Instead, she thought fast and said, "I would like to stay with Ross for a bit. He's in pain and he's my friend."

"Of course, but be home soon. I have a group who's taking him away to get him better."

She nodded at his lie. She knew Ross was being sent to train and he cannot train with broken limbs, the dumbass. People cleared out and before she knew it, she was alone with Ross.

"I'm in so much pain, Arden! I don't know what to do."

Arden looked around. She took off outside to see how many people were still in the arena. It turned out that the A Team ended up winning again. People were gathering their belongings and heading to their homes. Ellery spotted Arden outside the building. It was now dark. Ellery came up to Arden and hugged her. "You, I have a task for you." Ellery looked confused but agreed. "Here's your task. Wait here with him. Don't let anyone take him."

Ellery nodded. A few minutes had passed when Arden returned with a phoenix walking behind her on a leather leash. "What in the blue sky are you doing with that inside here?"

Arden did not answer but said, "Help me put Ross on the bird. I've recruited Dekker's help."

On the count of three, they lifted him up, laid Ross across the red bird's back, and strapped him in. They took a few deep breaths.

"What do you think you are doing?" Dekker asked suspiciously.

"What do you think? I am taking Ross to Earth. The humans have doctors who can help him because Adao won't help him."

Dekker stared at Ellery, not knowing what to say or do. They just looked at each other, daring the other do something about it. "So we are helping you escape against the king's wishes?" Dekker looked scared. The group would be there soon to get Ross. It is not happening. Not today.

"Just go! I am taking him to get healed and drop off this damn enrollment form since he can't deliver it now."

They slowly stepped back from her as she jumped up on the phoenix and checked on Ross once more. He was fast asleep. She closed her eyes for a moment to picture the route to the Chillicothe town on Earth. She needed to land in the same place as last time. She squared her shoulders and made the red bird walk out of the building. The night air felt cool to her sweaty skin. She wore just a bloody robe and hope on her face. She put a hand on Ross to steady him and one hand on the saddle. "Thank you." As her phoenix lifted in the air, she muttered, "Earth, here I come."

Chapter 4

BLACKNESS, STARS, AND red feathers were all she seen as she whipped by, trying to dodge the hovering warriors. She had darkness on her side and the element of surprise. No one expected to see some girl flying, especially at nighttime. Females are not warriors, therefore they do not fly. King Adao had strictly forbidden it. *Whoosh!* The wind rushed past as she cut through it. She had some difficulty maneuvering and remembering her trail.

Arden had landed like a novice, but the fact that she had arrived on the Earth's ground in one piece was an accomplishment. She said a quick prayer in her head and made sure Ross was still in tow. The saddle straps kept him secured. Her eyes wandered around and realized it was like seeing a new place again, a foreign world still. There were no people around, no strange aromas or loud noises. Just the whistle of the wind and a few lanterns here and there. She inhaled deeply to steady herself. Never has she felt so vulnerable and anxious. *Now what?* It is not as if she knew anyone to ask for help. What if she knocked on people's doors or screamed for help, would she be killed like her family was? It was almost certain there were more "spitters" out there. And Ross, he was a sitting duck, in all honesty.

Her blue-feathered head looked up toward The Sky to see if she was being followed. Nothing in sight. She could not help but give a small smirk of victory. She outsmarted The Fleet, at least for now. They will eventually be on the look-out for her, if not already. She knew she had to keep moving or she would be spotted from above.

The wind howled in the dusk and she heard some hooting sounds echoing amongst the trees. She assumed it was a bird,. now acutely aware that there are birds down here that she didn't know existed. Her breath was labored with fear and adrenaline. She slid off the phoenix in one fluid motion and looked around. Her poor bare feet stood on sharp, pointy gravel. "*Ow! Ow! Ow!*" she yelped in pain. She grabbed the leash and guided the red bird to walk with her. She led it on the only path that she knew, a dirt-and-gravel path that would turn into a cobblestone road. She noticed the stand where she got the enrollment form but it looked different in the shadows. Eerie. There were white tents hanging from some trees with humans occupying them. A hanging lantern cast their shadows on the nearby ground. She could hear some distant light chatter in the air. She knew she had to hurry. She darted along in survival mode. Moonlight shimmered on the road and provided the only comfort she was feeling. She shook her head no as if telling herself that this isn't right. In her dream, he told her to stay away, yet there she stood in complete despair.

She reached the porch area and stumbled on the step. Finally, every doubt that was replaying in her head immediately ceased. The wind was blowing her hair in every direction and she knew she would have to find courage.

She turned the tarnished knob but it was would not budge. Locked. She tapped lightly on the front door. Her hand shook as she kept looking over her shoulder to make sure no one would jump them. Humming a little melody to herself to calm her nerves, she tried knocking again. She didn't realize how much she relied on an able-bodied warrior. She always felt safe in their presence but then there wasn't all that much crime in The Sky to cause much fright. She pressed her ear to the door to see if music was playing. There was only silence booming loudly, almost as loud as her own heart. Nothing. She grabbed her head in disappointment and noticed she had a dull pain right in between her eyes. Anxiety began to build. She quickly turned around to look at the wounded warrior. "I need advice," she said aloud. She knew her only chance would be to wake Ross up from his slumber. She walked around the phoenix and tapped Ross on his good arm. She whispered in his ear and took the liberty of smelling his hair—a rugged, spicy scent. She lightly touched his tuft and pushed it back off his heated forehead. He moaned but was deep in sleep. She noticed he was turning black and blue all over his body. Dried up blood was on his outfit and caked on the tip of his nose.

"*Ahem!*" came a voice from behind her.

Arden jumped and armed herself with a water thermos. "Halt!" she yelled.

The person stood in the shadows and was taller than she was. "Well, if it isn't Bird Girl."

"Of all the people in the world who could have come to help us, it's you!" Arden crossed her arms and glared at her.

Spitter stepped forward aggressively. "Who the hell said anything about helping you? Why would I go and do a thing like that?" Her voice felt antagonizing and dark.

Arden dismissed that question. "What are you doing here? Do you live near The Hard Road?"

Spitter looked Arden up and down and laughed at the sight of her bare feet and laced dress. "This is my town, my neighborhood. As entitled as you may feel, you do not belong here. You are the outsider, beak face, who needs to fly away, like, pronto." Spitter was wearing a black cloth tied across her mouth. Only her nose and smoky eyes were visible.

Arden was close to just ending this exchange and try again somewhere else when the front door of The Hard Road jerked open.

"Tess, go home now," came a man's voice from the doorway.

"Fine. Do not even think about helping her, Myth. Don't!"

Tess (Spitter) continued walking down the dark street to an unknown destination as Arden stepped closer to the door.

"So you are Myth?" Arden asked weakly.

"I am no one. What are you doing here?" His voice was flat.

"Look, he's really injured. It's super late. We have no place to go. I know you hate us but—"

The man put his hand up and stepped to the side, allowing Arden and company to come through. The bar was as she remembered, but darker. The only light came from a back hallway, which, she assumed, was where his living quarters were. The man shut the door behind them. She realized it had to be the stranger, seeing how he owned the place and Tess had called him "Myth." He turned a small light on near the bar. That was just enough light to confirm her thoughts.

It was Stranger! She swallowed hard and took a deep breath. Her dream flooded her head and became feeble. She resented it. Those eyes that haunted her are right in front of her, in reality. She wanted to panic. She needed air.

"What happened?" he asked. She pointed at Ross who was strapped to the red bird. Stranger walked over to look at him and shook his head. "I know him. He comes here from time to time."

"So you are Mythias, the owner?"

He walked up close to her and looked down at her lovely blood-stained face. He did not say anything for a moment as if he was thinking. He became defensive. "How did you know I was the owner? You have only been here once."

So he remembered her, she knew it. Her heart was beating heavily. She decided to be blunt and honest. "I asked. Your drink maker told me."

He nodded but continued to glare. "My drink maker is called a bartender." *Man, what is up with the attitude and the staring?* As if he read her mind, he muttered, "Sorry. I have just not seen one of you up this close. Odd." That comment made her feel like they were on opposing teams and she was the enemy. "I will send for a doctor, although don't get your hopes up. People study down here but there are no degrees anymore. Hopefully he's practiced well for your boyfriend's sake." Relief flood over her. She had more confidence in this doctor-person than he did. *Wait, boyfriend?* She went to set him straight, but Stranger disappeared into a back room. She decided to sit down on a stool and take in the place. A few minutes later, he reappeared with a scowl on his face. "Want a drink while you wait for the doctor?"

"*Um*...sure, thank you." He grabbed a glass from the shelving area and made her mead. "I didn't give you my order, *bar-ten-der*." She exaggerated the word.

"If memory serves me, it's honey mead in a glass?" She was impressed.

"He's not my boyfriend," she blurted out.

He smirked but continued making the drink, which was just as beautiful as she remembered. He placed it in front of her and pulled a bottle of what they called beer from what appeared to be a cold box. He tipped it back and took a long, satisfying drink. She studied him. The way his neck stretched, and his odd human hands intrigued her. She couldn't help not to gape. He was the best-looking, most mysterious person she ever laid eyes on. His brown eyes met hers, this time he retreated.

A loud banging at the front door caused her to jump back to reality. Ross was hurting. *Ross, remember him, idiot?* She quickly made her way to the front door and discovered the doctor. To her surprise, a young man of about age twenty-five came through the entrance. She expected to see someone who looked like her wise and aged warriors who donned long white hair and fine wrinkles on their faces.

Instead, he had short light hair and pair of emerald green eyes that she had not seen before. So far, she had seen blue, brown, and green eyes. All Sky Walkers had blue eyes so this was an oddity. She wouldn't be surprise to see someone with yellow eyes!

The doctor carried a clear, see-through bag that he placed on a nearby table. It had different instruments, bottles, and medicines inside. "What happened?" he asked. Arden explained what had happened to her friend. Her voice was breathy and full of worry. *What if all this effort was for nothing?* "*Wow*, rough night! *Oh*, where are my manners! By the way, I am Koy. I'm a doctor who specializes in gastroenterology but am very capable of assisting him. He will be my first Sky Walker patient though so I can't promise that he will react to medicine correctly."

Arden smiled at him. "Thank you, Dr. Koy. We appreciate your help more than you know."

Koy touched Ross' face to get a temperature. He stood back and looked at Mythias. "Hey, Myth! You have an extra bed for this guy temporarily?"

Mythias gave a short "yes" then dashed into the back hallway. They could hear him cleaning a room and shuffling things around. Arden made her way down the hallway and saw him making a bed so she asked if she could help. She felt guilty, like they were putting him out. He didn't say anything but continued working. This man was quick with everything he did. Fast-paced, fast hands. He turned down the blanket and asked her to get a glass of cold water. Finally, something she could help with. It was a mundane task but a task nonetheless. She did as he asked and set the glass down on the side table next to a framed picture. Shock hit her when she saw Mythias' arm around a girl, Spitter. They looked happy and young in that picture. Confusion swept over her, she couldn't believe that they had been together. She is not sure why she would even care but it hurt her heart slightly. She walked back to Koy and Ross.

"We need to lay him down. He must be extremely uncomfortable."

Arden grabbed the leather leash and nudged them down the hallway into the guest room. The red bird, Arden finally read the nameplate, was named Char. His talons scratched the wooden floor as he strutted through to the bedroom. Koy, Arden, and Myth picked up Ross and laid him comfortably on the bed with a fluffy pillow supporting his head. Koy got out a green glowing tube of cream from the clear bag. With gloved hands, he began carefully rubbing the glowing ointment all over Ross's body, which gave him a green tint. The doctor then propped the broken leg up and began wrapping a thick white bandage around his entire leg. He did the same with the broken arm. Arden's curiosity got the better of her and had to ask about the glowing green gunk. "It's called aloe-healer. It is aloe that absorbs into the body and helps take pain away through contact. It zaps inflammation pretty quickly…at least on a human, it does."

She thought on it for a second. "The aloe that I know of is for dry and burnt skin. We put it on our phoenixes when they get burnt by their fire. I didn't realize it had this potential though."

Koy chuckled. "Yes, well, we adjusted and enhanced its molecules. Just think of it this way, it is an advanced aloe with a hundred times more potency. It will help heal your boyfriend. He will not be green forever either. It should wear off in time."

She grunted. "Why does everyone think he's my boyfriend? He is a childhood friend." Koy and Ross smiled at each other and looked unconvinced.

The doctor spent another thirty minutes cleaning out cuts. Arden wanted to wake him up so he would know that he was in good hands but she knew he needed sleep to mend. Koy left and promised to visit early in the morning. He even promised to bring some drinks called coffee-cola that Arden had not heard of before. It was 3:00 a.m. by this time. Arden didn't want to call it a night just yet even though her body was begging, especially not when she finally had face time with Mythias. She closed the guest room's door and joined Myth at the large table in the bar.

"Thank you again," she said in her meek and scratchy voice. As tiring as this day was, she felt alive.

He was sitting down and trying to finish his now not-so-cold beer. He motioned for her to go get her drink. She found her way around the kitchen area rather well and came back a short time later with her favorite drink in hand. "What about some music? I don't know how to work your high-tech device over there." He walked over to a wall beam that had a black panel that happened to control the music. Arden was a bit confused because Adao banned most technologically advanced systems. *How did he have such a thing?* He hit a button and a soft slow song came on. It was good background noise. He looked tired and a little rugged in a flannel shirt. He ran his hands through his hair. His eyes looked weak with dark circles under them. He sat down. "Why was there no one here earlier?" she wondered aloud.

"I closed on Sunday nights. I still honor our old ways, at times. Call me old-fashioned, I suppose. May I ask you a question now? Why the blue feathers? You dye them or something?"

That was a good question. Arden explained how she didn't know why. She grabbed a roped hair tie from around her wrist and began placing her disheveled hair into a high ponytail with tendrils hanging down to frame her face. Her eyes glistened in the darkened room and she felt her face heat up. Was it from the mead or him? She was not sure. "My turn," she said. "Why do you have a picture of Spitter in your guest room?"

"Spitter?" He laughed. "Are you talking about Tess?"

Arden did not find any of this funny. She was her sworn enemy and she felt like taking her down. "I call her Spitter because she spat in my face for making eye contact with her the first day that I came here. You may want to keep her off the welcoming committee, I'm just saying. And she doesn't seem at all your type."

He scratched the side of this neck and the smile faded. "Well, let's just say that Tess has been through a lot. No excuses, but she is a unique person for a reason. Everybody has a story." Arden was silent for a moment. "My turn. What do you think of King Adao?"

Her face grew serious. She didn't know what to say exactly about the king. She had mixed feelings about her uncle at this time. "Well, I *have* to support him."

He tried to comprehend her words. "Really? Why would you support such a dictator?"

"He is my uncle, after all."

His expression instantly went dark and spilled his beer loudly on the table. He adjusted himself in his seat. "You're his fucking niece?" he hissed.

She felt the anger, it was a palpable mass of heated pressure. The word *fucking* was not in her vocabulary, but it had a bite to it. "Yes, my father was—"

"Oswin was your father," he announced to his graffiti wall. His voice carried throughout the bar.

She was meek at first but felt a bit of fire burn inside. "Yes, King Oswin was my father. I loved my father. What does that matter anyway?"

He shifted his weight and then spun around to face her. "Of course that matters! Not only are you one of them, but you are directly related to my people's enemy, Adao." He took a breath then continued, "I want no one related to that tyrant in my house *and* he's going to be looking for you and I don't need him coming around here, that's for damn sure! So you need to go. No way around it. You go. You go first thing tomorrow morning, got it?"

For a moment, he reminded her of a red bird full of angst. She barely swallowed down the lump that was in her throat. "Fine, I will leave early. I have school tomorrow anyway."

Mythias stalked off to a hidden closet to get some blankets and a pillow. He threw a large cotton blanket on top of the big table. He moved their drinks to the side and placed a second blanket down. It looked as though she was going to be sleeping on the table tonight. She was happy with that. She was ready to be alone now. "You will sleep here tonight but I need you gone by seven."

She felt like a child who had been punished and told to stand in the corner. She just wanted to crawl up and sleep forever in her dreamland, a place of hope and brilliance. A place that was not here. She hopped up on the table and got herself situated. As Myth was about to make his exit, she spoke lightly. "Thanks, Myth."

He stopped with his broad back facing her. "Good night, Arden."

She rolled over on her side and watched him standing still, facing away from her. With her head resting on the pillow in a solemn state, she felt she had to add a few more comments. In the purest of voices, she slowly stated, "One last thing, please understand that *your* people murdered the family that I loved so much. *Your* people took my father, mother, and baby brother away from me. You humans view us as the enemy and that is okay. I understand it, I promise you. Just don't think that you feel the hatred alone. I deeply reciprocate your hate." She turned away and squeezed her eyes shut tightly.

Arden couldn't know it but her message hit hard. He felt the sadness in her gentle statement. He also understood the underlining darkness in her calmness. He was too caught up in disliking the bird people to even think of their loss. She was right though, the humans were responsible for her family's deaths. He witnessed that day and will never forget it. It was considered a holiday to the humans and it was named Day of Quietus. The humans celebrate secretly when they can. He continued to walk out of the room.

"I know," he muttered. His voice was wispy and drained. Arden thought she heard a faint hint of remorse in that tone, which made her feel a bit better.

*****

Arden surfaced back to the cold, hard reality of her current life. She was sleeping on a bar table on Earth, still feeling mentally and physically exhausted. She didn't move because she heard some men whispering from behind her. It took her a second to realize that it was Koy and Myth having a somewhat heated conversation.

"Are you kidding me? I can't have him staying here that long! The last thing I need are Sky Walkers living here and Adao showing up. My business will be ruined, not to mention that I would try to kill him the moment I saw him. You know my history with all this. I don't want to do that!" Myth said sternly.

Koy responded, "Look, I'll move him to a different place when he's healed more. Friend, relax. If Adao knew where she was, then he'd been here already."

Mythias scoffed, "That means nothing. He could be tracking her down as we speak."

Arden decided that was her cue. She rolled over and moaned as her body stretched across the table.

"Hey, Arden, I brought you some coffee-cola. It will wake you up…guaranteed." Koy coaxed.

She clumsily rolled off the table and asked what time it was. "It's 6:30 a.m.," they answered in unison.

Her hair was everywhere and her eyes were swollen. She grabbed the warm coffee cup and inhaled the pleasant aroma of the coffee bean. She liked it and could see herself drinking it every morning if it tasted as delicious as it smelled. She peered down at the brown bubbling brew as she took her virgin sip. It was sweet yet bitter, warm yet spritzed. Different sensations overcame her mouth then she finally swallowed it down with a smile. "Thank you, Koy, for thinking of me. What exactly is this again?"

Koy was adjusting his boots when he answered, "It's coffee, a hot drink that gives you energy. It's mixed with a sparkling coffee-flavored water that is infused with many nutrients. One cup nearly gives you all the nutrients that you would need in a day, at least for a human. That kind of stuff is needed when food is growing scarcer here."

After freshening up, she walked out of the bathroom to see Ross. He was awake and looking out a window. "Ross!" She quickly sat down on the bed beside him.

A smile formed on his face as he looked her in the eye. "Arden!" He practically sang her name.

"I panicked after you fell. King Adao was going to send you away for training. You couldn't possibly train. Dr. Koy is helping you. You actually look a little less bruised today." She was looking over his skin.

He snickered, "Well, it's because I'm green." Arden assured him that it would fade and explained that it was just an aloe mix. "You better get to The University before Adao finds you missing. I'll be in even more trouble if he found out you took me here for treatment."

She nodded. "I'll come back later to check on you."

Arden went to walk out of the bedroom when Ross said, "You are crazy to have done all this, but I…thank you."

She grabbed her thermos off the bar counter and looked around for Char. Koy had disappeared and Myth was nowhere to be found. Her head was still reeling from yesterday. A holiday that she will never forget for many reasons. She was hesitating to walk outside because of the humans but she had to. She hoped to go unnoticed but she was sure that was impossible seeing she was a Sky Walker in a gold-and-blue lace evening dress.

The door creaked open and the heat hit her in the face. She looked from side to side but saw no one, including Char. *Where could that bird be?* She can't go home without him. Her bare feet took her back inside to find a back door, which led to the backyard. It wasn't very big. A few plants here and there with a little brick building in the back of the lot. The fences that surrounded the area were made of brick and were tall, giving it a very private and secluded feel.

"It's seven." Myth's voice came from behind her.

She turned to see him cleanly shaved and looking rather rested compared to her. He was wearing a plain white T-shirt, combat boots, and dark green military-type pants. "Where's Char?" she questioned.

Myth stepped outside to meet her. "Char is eating inside. I kept him in my bedroom all night. I was going to take him outside but didn't want any humans to see him."

Inside, she found Char standing near the front door as if he knew it was time to fly. She grabbed Char and headed out the door in silence. The stoned road was a little hot on her feet. She decided to ride Char to get to The Landing quicker. Humans were walking around now. She got some looks. Some showed confusion, some anger, and some bewilderment. Most ignored her though. The looks made her feel insecure. But this was not about her, it was about Ross and doing the right thing. Moreover, she would have to get used to this if she was planning on attending the camp here, after all.

The camp! She had totally forgotten about the submission. The Landing's shops and stands would be coming up so she would try to drop it off before heading out. They trotted through the wooded area and was getting closer to The Landing. So much was running through her head. She could not help but to get a little teary-eyed from the exchange last evening. She didn't realize the hate that existed for her family and her kind. She wondered if she could help the king find a happy medium so everyone would respect one another for there to be some kind of peace. Then she thought long and hard on how that would never happen. The *creator* of The Sky Laws would not waiver.

Suddenly, a figure yelled, "Halt!"

Arden pulled back on the leash to stop Char. There were Fleet warriors quickly surrounding her. They carried odd weapons and pointed the speared end to her face, nearly cutting it. They were menacing, judgment written on their faces. These warriors happened to be wearing face paint in odd patterns. Shock and fear ran down her body. Char acted like a spooked horse. It took everything that Arden had to control him. She looked over her shoulder to see a familiar face staring back at her, a disdainful face of a Sky Walker named Fletcher.

Chapter 5

"YOU! WHAT ARE you doing here?" Fletcher asked in an accusatory tone.

Arden stayed on Char and spoke loudly above him. "I should ask you the same question. Is this necessary?" She pointed at his armed posse.

He seemed so serious. Different. "I'm running this post today, Miss Kress. Patrolling the area with my group, an area that you have no business being in. What in the hell are you doing down here?" He not only looked angry, he looked confused.

"Are you going to run and tell my sister now? Or better yet, the king?"

He kicked the dirt with his foot and his hands were resting on his hips. She noticed that he had face paint on too. Weird. "I have not decided yet. Maybe you should give me details, Arden. You know you are not supposed to be down here."

She shook her head. "No, no details. Look, you have questions and I have questions for you. Let's meet later and discuss this. I'm going to be late for class if I keep this up with you."

He looked around to see who else was watching. He had an odd weapon in his hand she did not notice before and it startled her. A white piece of equipment that had blinking blue lights on it. “Fine. Meet me where?”

She thought for a second. “This exact spot, nine o’clock tonight?”

He exhaled loudly but nodded and let her go. Arden regained her composure and took another long hard look at these painted Sky Walkers she had never seen before. *Buffoons!* Who were they and why are they stationed here? She had many questions that she would have to put on ice until tonight. She and Char were on their way again.

The Landing was busy and active this time of the day. People were standing in lines to get loaves of cinnamon bread for breakfast. The sweet aroma of baked goods and coffee-cola was all around, she was half tempted to join that line. She did not have money or a way to barter like the Land Roamers. People were setting up their booths and stands and dragging signs out that read “FRESH EGGS HERE” and “WILL BARTER FOR BEER.” The humans had limited food resources, Arden remembered from the museum tour. They trade services or goods mostly to get by. Since Adao banned boats most recently, it was more difficult for anglers to fish. The good fish were rarely near shore. Arden took a quick drink of her healthy coffee concoction and then spotted the camp stand on her left. She slid off Char and looked around. There were domed holograms showing videos of past campers and the activities they completed. Sky Walkers were smiling, laughing, and learning. Brochures and pictures were spread out on a dusty table manned by a strange man with one eye and a strong-smelling drink in his hand. She grabbed a brochure and finally seen the little girl come up to her. The human girl was wearing a cotton skirt with knee-high boots. Black ribbons were braided throughout her long hair. Her face was a mixture of glitter and dirt. Her feeble hands were carrying a big clear jar that read "Submissions." Arden smiled at her and dug for her paper to turn in.

"Good day. How are you today?" Arden asked while dropping her submission letter in the jar. Finally, mission accomplished.

The little girl smiled up at her. "You are very pretty. I like your nose."

A chuckle escaped Arden's smiling lips. She found out that the little girl's name was Ivy. "What? That's a coincidence. Ivy is my middle name. Can you believe it?" Ivy gave a toothy grin.

She thanked her for the entry and told Arden that the camp will be starting in a week from today. A packet of papers was placed in Arden's hand to keep and review. Details about the camp, such as what to wear, what to expect, and what foods will be provided. All the important details. The little girl asked if she could hug her. Arden stretched her arms out and gently held her. She wished that she could take her home to The Sky. Ivy asked if she could pet Char.

As the little girl's hands touched the side of the red-feathered bird, Arden's elbow was snatched pulling her to the hard ground. A painted warrior stood strongly above her. "Phoenixes are not pets. Use your head, Sky Walker!"

The warrior then shoved Ivy, making her fall backward. He demanded she get back to her stand immediately before he used the "nummer."

Arden realized that the nummer was the same white contraption Fletcher had. Arden steadied herself and pushed the warrior back from behind. "Do not touch her!" she commanded.

He then turned around and punched Arden in the face. Screams were heard and became an echo in the back of Arden's mind as she seen only rings of darkness.

*****

Arden rose with a throbbing headache and a package of ice resting on her forehead. She jumped to action, her wide eyes quickly accessing the place. She was locked in a small room with a rectangular window, a bedside table, and a brown bed. That arse knocked her out! She could not believe it. *Something is very wrong here,* she thought. The Fleet's warriors were acting out. *Why are so many of them roaming the street?*

Her tongue found a good-sized cut on her upper lip as she tried finding someone to let her out of the locked room. She dabbed her robe to her mouth to soak the rust-colored blood. It stung. "Let me out!" she yelled in a deep and forceful tone. After some minutes, she realized that no one was coming to check on her. The table had a vase of flowers on it. They were beautiful despite her situation. Thinking quickly, she took the pillow and placed it in front of her face. She grabbed the vase next and with all her might, she threw the vase through the window, the glass shattered loudly. Then she hopped on the table and yelled, "HELP!" The window faced an alley where bricks were her only view. What an unhelpful sight.

All of a sudden, the sound of loud footsteps rapidly approached the room. Her door swung open, hitting the wall. She jumped off the table and balanced herself. A large Sky Walker stood in the doorway with an angry face, the face of King Adao. Arden gasped and quickly sat down on the bed.

King Adao walked in the room and stared her down with burning fury. A feeling of panic and doom lingered over her. "Arden, we leave now." He grabbed her sore arm and dragged her down hallway after hallway as fast as he could.

Chapter 6

LATER THAT NIGHT, her tear-stained face laid upon her pillow as she reflected on the scuffle. Such turmoil, excitement, and hurt. She had stretched her mind and body beyond what she thought was possible this past week, a soup of emotions. She would have thought it was only a dream, but the rug burns on her knees and thighs were proof enough. She disobeyed, which she felt immense guilt over but relished in it at the same time. As part of her punishment, Arden is not allowed outside her bedroom for three weeks. Loki, the head cook, is to drop off meals and leave immediately.

Arden sat on her comfy bed but could not get comfortable knowing that Ross is down on Earth with Mythias and she was far, far away in The Sky. She's supposed to meet Fletcher at nine this evening. She missed school, which saddened her too. Everything was flipped upside down. Her world feeling like a labyrinth that she will never conquer. Her legs felt heavy as she walked across the room before she plopped lazily on her golden bed. With nothing to do but feel sorry for herself, she decided to read. Her eyes scanned the beautiful built-in bookshelves stacked with books from floor to ceiling. The glistening cobwebs in the ceiling corners were inevitable. Glass figurines and Ravel Reed items were placed in an organized manner. Despite the books, she kept everything else very tidy. She stood up and viewed them with pride. She loved her books. They were part of her soul. They were the vessels of written journeys. Rubbing her reddened nose, she walked around the room and grabbed her glass of lukewarm water. "If this is my prison for three weeks, then so be it," she stated out loud, putting her hands on her hips. She could think of worse that is for sure.

Nighttime rolled around, visions of Adao's face haunted her. She couldn't sleep knowing people were wondering where she was and she worried about Ross' health. Adao took her domed bracelet so she couldn't' message anyone. She recalled for a moment when they landed and got to the estate. He was direct with her and asked the expected questions, What were you doing down on Earth? How did you get there? What was going through your head, ignorant girl? She told him that she took it upon herself to bring down the submission slip since she had forgotten to submit it on the field trip. His frustrated response was, "You are *never ever* to go down there again! You disrespected our kind by letting a human touch one of our phoenix. Humans are to fear them, not regard them as pets. That's called superiority." Before he left her, his final words were, "No camp for you. You are to reside in this estate for three weeks. I will have Aspen send for your classwork. And in case you were wondering, yes, Daughter, you are truly a disappointment." Then he walked away and carried on with his day. That last comment left her breathless.

The next morning, she slept in since her body needed the rest. She made a plan in her head for the day while grabbing the heated breakfast tray outside her bedroom door. It consisted of books, classwork, and devising an escape so she can make it to the camp. She ate her food and admired her window view. The University stood not too far away from her house. She did miss it, along with her friends and Miss Emory. Lost in her thoughts, she noticed a speck was making its way closer and closer to her lane. She noticed it was a person walking toward the estate, a male in a warrior outfit. Her heart stopped briefly, thinking it was Ross. *Could it be? Did the aloe-healer work already?* His back was to her as he made his way to the front door. She could not tell who it was. Twiddling her thumbs, she waited to see if she would have a visitor. She picked her clothes quickly and set her food tray down on the bathroom counter. She made her bed in twenty seconds flat. The anticipation grew as well as her impatience. Ten minutes passed, she marched back over to her window in disdain. She felt lost, like Lady of Shalott locked up in her tower, and it had only been one day!

Something hit the window, making Arden flinch. She glared out looking for the culprit. She saw the warrior throw another rock at her window, waving his arms in the air. It was Fletcher without the face paint. She opened the window. "Meet me in the gardens, the fifth nest on the right," he said before he took off.

After flitting through hallways and taking secret passages like a professional, Arden made it to the gardens in no time. Luckily, no one saw her. She ran as fast as she could to the fifth tree. Her hands and feet moved fluidly up the tree ladder to the nest on top. Fletcher and Red, the warrior from the field trip, were sitting in the nest, quietly waiting on her. Arden found a spot and sat down with labored breath. She noticed the relaxed mood on their faces. "So as you were probably told, I'm housebound for three weeks. I couldn't meet you last night."

Fletcher stated he had heard about the incident from his father, the head warrior. "Everyone is talking about it. Walkers cannot believe that you stole a phoenix and went to Earth without a warrior. You of all people, Arden. It was a slap in your uncle's face. It was reckless. You know that, right?" She shook her head and decided not to argue. "Well, that explains why I bumped into you."

"Yes, now you know why I was there. But I need to know why *you* were there. I also want to know why you were painted up and with a group who threatened me." She inched a little closer to them, enjoying the conversation after being alone for some time.

"Well, if I tell you something, you must promise me that you will not repeat this. I am serious, Arden. This is serious as serious goes. My life could be taken for divulging this, but I feel…*um,* I feel like you should know what your uncle is running." She assured him that she would not repeat his words ever. A feeling of great worry came over her. She knew that what she was about to be told was going to change her in some way. He took a deep breath and began. He told her about the top secret information, Class X, he called it. Fletcher said that King Adao has hundreds of warriors stationed at different posts, in the air and on the ground. "There are three types of warriors in the army. The Scouts are the warriors of the ground. They wear signature face paints. The Sky Walkers do not know about us. As I am sure you could guess it, I'm a Scout. The second group is called The Scopers, the warriors of The Sky. They scope out crime. Red here is a Scoper." He pointed at Red who sat quiet but looked proud and accomplished. "They are the typical warrior that everyone knows about, the kind of warrior we all pretend to be. The third type—and the most dangerous—are called Strikers. They are handpicked special warriors of torture and holding. They judge the humans and work closely with King Adao on the best way to punish them. They use very disturbing ways to accomplish this. You can tell they are Strikers by a roped tassel around their right bicep." Fletcher stopped to clear his throat and began again. "Once they are snatched up, they are taken to High-Rise Fortress to be judged. There are two options for a captured human, to be killed immediately or be tortured and jailed in the fortress for the rest of their life. No human comes back from the High-Rise." His eyes and hands were animated as he was talking. "There's a secret section in The Sky Laws that describes this justice. I am just glad I'm not a Striker. I dislike humans but I cannot torture someone like that. It's not in me."

Arden absorbed his every word. "I'm glad you aren't a Striker too. What was your father before he became The Fleet leader?"

Fletcher stood up to take a good look at The Sky and make sure they were not being watched. He seemed a little paranoid. "He was a Striker. He reminds me of that all the time. He feels dishonor in my ranking, I think." His blue eyes looked empty for a moment before he quickly sat down on the straw.

Red finally spoke up. "I fully support Adao. Humans are unpredictable. Not sure if you know this, but humans pollute the Earth. They are the sole reason the atmosphere heated up, causing partial global warming because of the greenhouse gases. Do you know what that means for us? If King Adao had not stepped in and made us control them, then we would have acid rain in our clouds right now. It just so happens to be life threatening to all Sky Walkers. The Sky Laws are applied to everyone but strict repercussions occur should a human not abide. Hell, once a human girl was killed because she stole some bread one morning. Now is that extreme? I believe so." This made Arden think of Ivy, praying that she was not taken. Hopefully, they were too focused on Arden to punish the girl. She asked if the humans were aware of the different types of warriors. Red said, "No, they don't know. They see us as one united army. We are just The Fleet to them."

Arden struggled a little because she was lied to by her uncle, but he was lying to everyone else, also. Was the idea of a prison a big deal? No. Was the idea of torturing people over small crimes a big deal? Yes. Arden had a big problem with that indeed. She felt bits of anger flicker from inside her. After an hour, Arden became a bit antsy, hoping that no one had gone to her room to check on her. She thanked Fletcher and Red for coming to see her. They were a nice distraction despite their dark words.

"I'll come visit you again soon," Fletcher promised.

He and Arden have never been close before, but she now seen him in a different light. He wasn't some snobby, rank-given kid like she originally thought. She liked the promising colors he showed her today and the utter honesty. He also trusted her with classified information. She hugged them both and then sprinted for her room.

******

With hours stretching before her, she searched through her books and found an old paperback she hadn't seen before tucked away on a shelf. As her hands felt the cold cover, she decided to breathe in the history of it, dust and all. Sitting down on a blue empire chair, she opened the mysteriously hidden book titled *Vintage Lovely* written by Cokie Alexander. When she opened the book, she noticed a short message in cursive writing. "This book belongs to M. E. Cottonwood." The title itself was confusing. Then it hit her that this book was a human book. Adao must had taken it from Earth. Excited, her mouth dropped open and eyes widened. Now she has plenty of time to read this book. A bonus to imprisonment!

It was two o'clock in the morning when she closed the book. She read straight through it and realized she needed a snack. She was starving and wide awake after all that love talk. Popping sweet grapes in her mouth, she pondered on the interesting human literature that was just consumed. It was a compilation of the greatest love stories of their history. It made her heart beat fast and yearn for something she did not understand. Some died for love and some people killed for it. A strong emotion, she realized, that frequently became someone's motivation. *Does romance still exist in their current world?* Sky Walkers, of course, have sex and reproduce, but they do not speak about that type of thing typically. Ravel Reed does write about love but he doesn't describe the sexual acts. It is considered unlawful and distasteful. *Wow!* She was happy she found it. "Crazy humans!" she stated aloud with a smile on her reddened face.

Chapter 7

ARDEN WAS COMPLETELY restless with the same old routine day in and day out. She had not heard from Fletcher—or anyone, for that matter. She had been left out of everything! Thumbing through a calendar book, she remembered that camp would be starting in two days so she had to act on her plan very soon. *Today.* She decided she was going to sneak out and go to Earth early to spend time with Ross. How long would she last before her overprotective uncle would come searching with a vengeance, she didn't know. But knew she *had* to go because her trust in King Adao was starting to crumble away as her yearning for Earth began to grow wildly.

She gathered her belongings in a big brown shoulder bag with her initials AIK (Arden Ivy Kress) sewn on the backside. She had clothes, jewelry, lip shine, a Ravel Reed novel, *Vintage Lovely*, and milo seed—all the essentials a young female Sky Walker would need. She began to wonder if her dear friends, Ellery and Dekker, were going to this camp too. She decided to write a letter the old-fashioned way on paper and leave it in her room. She wanted to express to King Adao that she does love him; but must learn more about the beings that they have full custody over.

> Dearest Uncle,
>
> I need you to understand my being gone against your wishes. I must make sense of these beings that we control, therefore I must fully experience Earth. I need the freedom to do this. I do promise you this, Uncle—I will never disobey you again. Ever.
>
> Please forgive me. I will return in two weeks after camp is over. No later.
>
> Yours truly,
> Arden Ivy Kress

Arden sealed the letter and placed it on her wrinkled pillow. She exhaled loudly. Her hand shook as she thought of disobeying the king again. She wasn't just playing with fire, but a full-blown firestorm. Not too wise. But Arden found herself being more and more rebellious and she was not quite sure why. Maybe it was finding out information that made her feel differently about The Sky Laws and her uncle. Maybe it was a newfound freedom that only the humans had inspired. She felt there was something greater. Fate was leading her on her path of knowledge and empowerment and she did not want the detour route.

With her bag in tow, she secretly made way to the gardens knowing that was the easiest and safest escape route. The cool breeze hit her face, it felt lovely. She closed her eyes and breathed it in for a moment. Her sandaled feet brought her near the backwoods toward The University. She couldn't go that way since it was the busiest place in The Sky. She headed toward the warrior's stable area instead. She knew she had to steal a phoenix to revisit Earth. She carefully opened the big iron gate that led to the muddy training grounds. Hiking up her skirts, she ran for the nearby stables. Voices of warriors echoed through the air. She doubted for a second whether it was too late to go back. She ran low to the ground. Hunched over, she peeked around corners until the large stable area was about a hundred yards away. She took off faster than ever. She was on a mission. Up ahead was an empty area where some chained up red birds were. She was finally face-to-face with the birds. She quickly read the nameplates around their collars. She wanted Blaze or Char as she ran down each aisle. Eventually, she found Char. As he made eye contact with her, there was recognition in his beautiful golden eyes. He looked elated to see her. Patting him on the back, she whispered to her dear friend, "Just like before, Char. Just like before." She unchained his scaly leg and walked him out of the stable.

"HALT!" yelled a male's voice from the back. She turned her head slightly to face the warrior. "Where do you think you are going?"

She fumbled on her words, trying to come up with a good excuse. "I was just taking him out to get bathed. Yeah, he's…*uh*, dirty." She blurted out the first thing that came to mind. She heard laughing. She then fully turned to see the warrior and to see what was so damn funny. It was Fletcher.

He laughed again. "Arden, really, what are you doing?" He stepped closer to her.

She smiled. "I have got to, Fletcher. Will you help me?" He rolled his eyes in a playful way as if to say, "She's up to one of her tricks again." She declared, "I am going to camp."

His face became serious within seconds. "Adao approve that?" He already knew the answer to this as she was on house arrest.

"Save it!" she muttered. "I'm going with or without your help." Fletcher pushed his hand through his hair and exhaled loudly. Arden had a knack for putting people in odd situations and exhausting them. He did not like it but knew Arden enough that there was no use arguing with her, a lawyer in training. "Can you escort me to Earth for camp then come get me in two weeks? That is, if Adao doesn't have me killed." She injected a little humor in her voice in such a worrisome statement. She could tell he was reluctant but finally agreed to the plan.

"Fine. We better hurry then."

Fletcher brought Char out in the open. She accepted his help with mounting Char even though she didn't need it. He told Arden to hang on to her bag and, most importantly, him. The ride was easy and quick this time since Fletcher was an experienced rider. The landing was very smooth. The experience of flying was just as amazing as her first time. The place was chaotic with humans everywhere. Fletcher asked when the camp officially starts.

Arden had to confess that they were two days early. "What in the hell are you going to do for two days, Arden? It's not safe down here even with the Scouts around."

She saw his worried look and smiled. "I have a few friends down here. I wanted to see them before heading to camp. They will keep me safe." As they both jumped off Char, he wanted to know who her "friends" were. Arden refused to say. "One friend is one of us."

He looked even more confused. "Well, can I walk you to your 'friend'?"

She shook her head no and placed a small kiss of gratitude on his cheek, causing Fletcher to blush. "I'm going to walk. It is not far away, I promise. Plus, I have vulgar spray in my bag as a weapon."

He knew that vulgar spray was potent so he finally let her go. "Arden, please be careful and don't make me regret this. Have fun at your camp."

After repositioning the bag on her back, she fixed her robe that got wrinkled from the ride. "Go get your face painted, Scout."

She walked away with Fletcher watching her all the way from The Landing to around the corner where he had originally stopped her with spears just days ago.

Her head was clear. She felt great. She felt free. She could not wait to see Ross, Myth, and Koy at The Hard Road. When she got there, she slowly stepped up on the porch and opened the door without knocking. As the door creaked open, she was immediately hit with the familiar smell of the bar, a bit of smoke, dust, and alcohol. The bar area was empty. She wondered if everyone was up and awake yet. Dropping her bag on the counter, she made her way down the hardwood halls. Ross' door squeaked open. She peeked in to see him lying in bed. He did not look as good as she expected. He was still green and sweaty. She did notice that many of his bandages were gone though. She sat down on the side of the bed and looked at his sleeping face.

"Ross?" she whispered. He mumbled but did not move. "It's Arden." Still nothing. She looked around the room for a few seconds and saw a machine that she had not seen before. It looked like complicated medical equipment. She noticed that he was not wearing a shirt still and had cotton pants on. Myth's. They had "human" written all over them. She looked again at his face, a beautiful face that copied her hooked nose exactly. Her eyes trailed down to his chest. She was relieved to see no cuts or contusions. She continued to look at his muscular frame and defined arms. Her body froze.

No! No, he cannot be! A roped tassel was dangling from his right bicep, a tassel that represented a warrior who tortures, judges, and kills. Ross was a Striker!

Chapter 8

ARDEN'S THOUGHTS ECHOED loudly through her mind as she pulled up a bar stool in the main area. She ran her fingers through her long hair and rubbed her scalp for some relief. Disappointment rained down upon her. Betrayal burned in her in an unexplainable way. She never expected Ross, a good-natured and charming Sky Walker, would be a warrior who tortured people. He was a paid murderer! This newfound information rattled her and made her wonder what else was being kept from her and her people.

She worked her way around the kitchen, made her fizzy nutritious beverage, and then headed for the table that served as her bed that vulnerable night from mental and physical exhaustion. She patted the table as if to say, "Hello, my friend. I missed you."

Arden could hear footsteps coming down the hallway but she continued drinking as if she lived there. Mythias came around the corner and headed to the kitchen area, not noticing the coffee-stealing intruder sitting at the table. His hair was sticking up in places as he began stretching his arms. She kept quiet until the right moment. He looked to be making breakfast, but Arden did not know the ingredients he was using. She could tell that he had eggs but she was not sure what he was going to do with them.

"Ahem!" Mythias looked up from his stove and arched his defined eyebrows. She was expecting a smile of some sorts but she did not get it. Her disappointment slowly faded. "Arden, where have you been?"

She stood up and walked to the bar. She loved the way he said her name. "I've been on house arrest. I was caught at The Landing the day I left here. It went badly, Myth. I got a busted lip and a nice little visit from my uncle." She rolled her eyes. He began frying the eggs but was still listening intently. "What are you doing? You do realize that's a baby bird, right?" Her voice trembled as she watched the yolk sizzle on the frying pan. Her hand came up to cover her mouth.

"No, the baby bird hasn't developed yet. No baby bird, I promise you." He made eye contact with her.

She swallowed. "Anyway, about Ross. He does not look good. What's going on?" she asked. Mythias told her that he would explain Ross' health over breakfast shortly. "What kind of eggs are you making?"

"Isn't it obvious? Chicken eggs." He chuckled.

"Chicken? I've not heard of them."

"So the Bird Girl doesn't know about birds, *huh*?"

"I do know about *my* kind of birds. You must have different ones than we do. Ross and I will not eat that, just so you know."

He slid the lightly peppered eggs over easy on his plate. "I will make you chia seed pancakes with syru, then. No one can buy maple syrup these days, but I make a good substitution."

"You had me at *chia seed*." They both burst out laughing.

"Of course you like seeds."

He had a playful look on his face and seemed rested. Normal, even. The pancake batter had already been mixed and was now becoming fluffy little cakes. Arden got the forks out of the drawer and set the table. Ross was still in slumber when she joined Myth at their nice little breakfast setup. It looked lovely, and the vase full of white daisies made it feel homey too.

"This does look good, I must say." She took her first bite of the pancakes.

"As for the pancakes, no bird was harmed in the making of these." He sniggered. Arden asked about Ross. "Koy will be able to explain it better. If I remember correctly, Koy said that he had an allergic reaction to the compound that activates the healing component in the aloe-healer. Koy had to stop the aloe-healer so Ross is healing slowly and in pain. Broken bones are hard to heal on their own. Turns out, he has some other issues going on too, like high blood pressure. Again, Koy is the doctor, he can explain it in better detail. But in the end, Ross will be just fine."

Arden exhaled loudly. That is all she wanted to hear. Her good friend will be "just fine."

After breakfast, Arden began putting the dirty dishes in the sink and cleaning up. Myth went to take a quick shower. She went back to Ross' room. He was awake in bed, his eyes focused on a window. "Hey, you," she said in a half whisper.

Ross turned his head and smirked. "Boy, am I happy to see you! Where have you been, lush?"

"Good to see you haven't lost your sense of humor." She explained where she had been and what had happened with her uncle. He was worried that Adao would come looking for him since he was MIA. Arden assured him that he was safe. Even though they were conversing in such a natural way, she was tempted to tell him that she knew about him being a Striker. She would never do so because she gave her word to Fletcher and she would never dishonor that. She did not see any harm in asking him innocently what the tassel was though. She wanted to gauge his reaction. Her fingers went to his arm and played with the rope. "What is this? I've not seen this before." she asked nonchalantly.

He shrugged his shoulders, his face became placid. "Nothing. Just part of the warrior uniform."

Arden nodded in agreement. Playing innocent was an easy task for her. She couldn't read his face fully but she could tell there was a story there—a deep, dark story that he was guarded about. To lighten the mood, she offered to get him some honey mead and he took her up on that offer. She did not know if Dr. Koy would approve such a drink but she did not care. Making him feel better and happier was her top priority and duty as a friend. "Once a lush, always a lush."

After a full day of being with Ross and quizzing Koy, the night was upon them and Myth had a business to run. Arden developed a headache and felt like she needed some alone time so Myth gave her his room to rest in. He apologized for the noise ahead of time. She shut his bedroom door and looked around the rather tidy room. It was a man's bedroom, a room that felt foreign and forbidden to her. She smirked at all the manly things he possessed. He had many books that were stacked neatly. A patch collection was displayed on a long wooden desk, which appeared to be for military clothing. One patch said "Runner." Another patch had a picture of a knife with "We Stand" written in cursive below it. She liked that he collected something for a hobby. She compared it to the brooch collection that she cherished almost as much as her books.

For some reason, there were feelings stirring inside at the fact that she was going to sleep in the very place he does every night. She jumped on the bed in a childish manner and stretching her arms and legs out like an *X*. The cold sheets felt good on her bare feet. She rolled over to smell his fluffy white pillow. She breathed in a lovely scent, a heavenly mixture of soap, musk, and goodness. Without thinking, she buried her face into the pillow, inhaling deeply. She pulled back and shook her head in disdain. "What is wrong with you?" she scolded herself. She grabbed her brown bag and got her books out. Maybe tonight is not a good night to read *Vintage Lovely* since she was already off-kilter. She will admit that she got "hot and bothered" and she was also extremely annoyed by it.

*****

Woo! Bar noises woke her up in the middle of the night. She sat straight up and looked for the clock. It was 2:11 a.m. *These people are still going strong. Humans like to party no matter what is going on with the world.* She smiled at that. After yawning aloud, she stumbled to the light switch. She did not feel like going back to sleep so she decided to join the party.

Walking by a mirror, she realized that she could not possibly go out in her nighttime robe, it was too revealing. She quickly threw on a white T-shirt of his that read "Hanging by a Thread" and a pair of Myth's pajama bottoms. Her hair was tucked into a bun on top of her head. She walked down the hallway and entered the dimly lit bar area. Looking around, she saw humans everywhere. Some dancing, some singing, but all were drinking. She noticed Mythias was working the bar with the friendly person from her first day on Earth. "Hello, do you remember me?"

He turned to look at her and smiled. He had friendly and expressive eyes. "Why, yes, I sure do. You are Arden," he said in an accent that she wasn't familiar with.

"Good memory. You speak differently, I really like it."

He told her he was Irish, which did not really help her. She had never heard of the Irish but she was a huge fan already. She went behind the counter so she could join Myth.

"You're awake." He looked her up and down. "I see you found my clothes." Arden noticed a corner of the counter that had a pile of odd items resting on it: goggles, eggs, knives, towels, bowl of nuts, pocket watch, jewelry, apple pie, a leather bag, and some other items she hadn't seen before. She pointed at them and asked where they came from. "I barter for drinks. This is what people brought in tonight. I also take cash." He adjusted his shirtsleeves and looked around the bar. "Bout that time, friends!" he yelled. Everyone were putting down their drinks and headed out the front door.

Arden stood up and asked what the Irish fellow's name was. "Wickham. But you can call me Wick." She nodded.

"More like Wick-*ed*." Myth added in the background as he was cleaning up. Wick and Myth teased each other and acting as if they were going to fight but it was in a boyish, friendly way.

"Well, I'm going to gather my tips and be off, my friend." He patted Myth on the shoulder.

"Wait! Wick, I know you want to go home, but I have another question for you." There was seriousness in her voice that made Wick straighten up his posture a little more. He gave an "aye" for her to continue. "When I first met you, I asked you for Myth's name. Your response was, 'The lad's name is Mythias. Most call him Myth. Some call him Runner Boy. We call him the owner of this bar.' Do you remember that?" He did not know where she was going with this but nodded his head. "So my question is, why Runner Boy? I did see a patch with the word *runner* on it in his bedroom. Does that have anything to do with it?"

Wick's eyes grew worried. Before Wick could respond, Mythias came from the back room. "Runner Boy? You've been asking about me?" he questioned with hard eyes.

Arden felt small, like she was caught in some kind of childish, girly gossip. "*Um*...yes. It is an odd nickname is all. Never heard of such a name." She thought she played that off very well. She gave herself a small invisible congratulatory pat on the back.

Myth was second-guessing this discussion. "Look, Wickham, I'll explain it to her. It's my story to tell."

Wick shrugged and nodded before walking over to Arden. He gave her a quick hug and bid farewell for the night. Arden and Myth sat down at the big table, the indispensable table. Myth admonished Arden that if she wanted more information, just ask him directly instead of fishing for answers with others. That was fair. She settled in, pulling her knees up to her chest and sitting back in the uncomfortable wooden chair. She was ready for the personal story that he was about to tell.

"Actually, my back is killing me and I'm tired from work. Do you mind if we get comfy in my bedroom?" His eyes widened and he shook his head. "I mean, because I can actually rest my back compared to this hard-ass chair." Arden blushed as they made their way back to his bedroom. As he opened the door, to his surprise he seen a slinky, satin piece of clothing sprawled out on his bed. He closed his eyes for a second then grabbed the garment. His hands stroked the lace for a few seconds. "This yours?"

Embarrassed, she quickly snatched it up. "I think I found that in the back of your closet. Must be yours," she said snidely.

"Well, I think I prefer the T-shirt on you." He began looking her up and down with a fading smile, which turned a little dark. It made her heart skip a beat. He looked serious that she could not help but gulp. She didn't know how to take this. Did he really find her attractive, especially at this very moment in his ragged, Hanging by a Thread T-shirt?

"Make yourself comfortable, please." He took off his shirt slowly and stretched out on the bed.

Confusion clouded her mind. *What is this? Should they be this comfortable to lay half naked on the bed together at 2:35 a.m.?* Quickly, her mind tried to push through the clouds. One thing that could cut through these feelings of confusion was her body's response to him. It was natural, she decided to go with it. She slipped out of his pajama pants but kept the long T-shirt on. She thought to herself while looking down at her shirt, *Talk about hanging by a thread...that's me this very second.* She snickered to herself. Her long legs were glowing in the dull light. She was beyond happy that she remembered to put lotion on earlier that night. She walked around the bed and laid down, making eye contact with him. He had his pants on but she still felt vulnerable with his bare chest exposed. He was insanely handsome. The only male that she was super comfortable with was her best friend Dekker, but she still would not have worn this around him. He watched her in silence and did not dare look elsewhere. Shyness radiated from her as a small nervous smile played on her pink lips. She adjusted her blue-feathered head on the pillow to find a comfortable position. As they faced each other, the golden specs gleamed in his brown eyes, making her swoon quietly. His body heat was radiating. She had to fight the urge to pounce. She had difficulty swallowing but did not want to take her eyes off him either. His silent confidence intrigued and mesmerized her. She then rested her head on her arm and waited in great anticipation. He was about to get vulnerable with her, possibly tell her his life story. Noticing his silence, she reached out and touched his face for encouragement. It was only for a few seconds as she wanted him to feel calm. She quickly realized this did the complete opposite. She could see it on his face plain as day. He responded to that touch. He looked as if he had not been touched in a lifetime. His eyes were hungry as he inched closer to her as if she were a hot bright fire in the coldest of nights. Their legs were now touching.

"Wait," he said hesitantly. He took a long deep breath as if he was trying to steady himself. Caving into temptation, he ordered, "Come here."

Her body froze instantly, yet she felt herself growing hot at the same time. It felt like combustion was its only option. He said to come to him. *Get closer, fool!* she yelled inside her head. What was going to happen? She slid a few inches closer. Now her heaving chest was touching his. Breathing was becoming harder for her as she felt desire consume her. She thought it was what she was feeling and convinced that this feeling was mutual. She felt love drunk and could not get enough of this closeness. Insatiable desire.

Before she knew it, his rough hand was on her lower back, pulling her slowly to him. Her leg wrapped automatically around the side of this body, resting on his hip. They both gasped. His finger felt her hooked nose as he examined her face as though she were a masterpiece. No words were needed, just his eyes and body were enough. She could not help but notice that his jawline was graceful yet sharp and his face was flawless. No longer could she bear this feeling. She longed to kiss him, be with him. She made the first move. Her curved lips softly brushed his open mouth. His arid breath hit her hard. She did this repeatedly as if daring him to cross the line and kiss her. It worked. He began kissing her long and soft. Again and again. Over and over. Ragged breathing overwhelmed them both as they became a tousled mess of needy body parts. Her mind was in overdrive and her numb. She undoubtedly could do this all night long or for eternity. Her hands dared to cup his face as she pulled him harder to her. Lust lingered in the air as he finally found strength to pull away. The last kiss echo throughout them both, reverberating like a bell rang. Their panting was in sync. Giddiness. Bliss. Her ice blue eyes stayed locked onto his. She realized that she had her very first kiss. To top it off, it was with a human boy. It could be added to *Vintage Lovely* because that very moment was sexy as hell.

Chapter 9

ARDEN PULLED AWAY from Myth to adjust her now awkwardly stretched T-shirt. Waving her hands in front of her heated face, she softly blew air out of her mouth. They settled back to their original positions.

Myth cleared his throat and waited for his breathing to slow. "Runner Boy" He shook his head. "Let me go back further. It's about your family. I don't want to upset you…" he trailed off in thought.

Arden reached over and touched his hand. "It's fine. Whatever it is, I want to know."

"Well, I was about eleven years old when your family was killed. That day, we were getting food at The Landing. I can still remember the shock on my parents' faces when your family showed up. Let me explain something to you… when humans get scared, we get defensive, especially when being told we've been watched from above like some damn experiment. It was like a storm…everything happened so fast. Anyways, I witnessed the attack and saw your father get stabbed. We took off running as fast as we could back home after that." His solemn eyes examined Arden. "Most humans believe that killing Oswin was smart because he was probably like Adao. I used to believe that, but after meeting you…I'm not so sure." He rolled over on his back and looked at the ceiling. His profile became pronounced in the dim light.

"My father was nothing like my uncle. He had a heart of gold. He wanted to make a difference, but he was not given the chance to prove his intentions."

"King Adao banned weapons, electronics, airplanes, boats, and food. He flew loads of our food and weapons up to your land. We underestimated his power. We underestimated his warriors. Anyway, my point is that my parents, my older brother Marco, and I were held captive in our home for months. I remember my parents finally getting sick of it and planned to attack the warriors while we escaped out the back window. Their plan partially worked… they were both killed but we did escape."

Arden put a hand over her mouth, her eyes began to glisten with unshed tears. "How?"

"They were all burnt and cut up. Nummers, I suspect. When Marco and I came back, they were dead and the warriors were gone. We gathered up our belongings and took off again. We did horrible things to survive…" He cracked his knuckles and then continued, "Let me speed things up. So when I was sixteen years old, I had enough of Adao's crap. I witnessed this bullshit every single day. People getting beat up, set on fire, kidnapped. They also banished humans for the smallest of things. All I'll say is that suppressed anger is toxic to the mind and soul. I wanted to kill Adao. You have no idea of the hate within me." Darkness crept in his vulnerable eyes as he replayed what happened. "It became a goal of mine to save people and kill the warriors, a personal war that many others later joined. I helped build an army organized by a group of my friends and big brother. You probably don't know this, but we created an underground operation. We made our own weapons out of scrap metal though I never killed one of those fuckers—Sorry," he promptly apologized for his language. "My job title was Runner Boy. When I would see injustice, I would help the person escape 'running' them to our underground headquarters for safety. I used explosives to distract the birds, but they were too weak to do much damage. I was able to save only two people, all the others were taken into The Sky. We tried to run these people away from Adao's grasp but we fail repeatedly. I could not comprehend that this Sky Walker had so much power and I am powerless." He shifted his weight onto his right side and looked at Arden again. A vein began popping out of his neck as his eyebrows scrunched together.

"So you had your own top secret army, but why did you stop?" she asked.

"The reason I stopped was because my brother Marco was captured, trying to save another person. That's when I realized that this was not worth it anymore."

She offered, "I know that it feels like it wasn't worth it, but think of the two people you did save. You are still a hero in my eyes. I'm sure those two survivors think the same."

Mythias did not respond to the hero talk but continued as if she had not said anything. "I had a mental breakdown and shut down the operation. I rallied my friends and vowed that we watch after ourselves and our families from here on out. That was it. We had to admit defeat and, ultimately, resolve to no longer 'run' people to safety. So now we don't."

Arden laid in silence as she allowed the story to sink in. 'I'm so sorry about Marco. I understand. Like you, I lost my parents and brother." She sat up with a serious look on her face. "By the way, I saw your patch collection. Now it makes sense that it was for your army. Is that why 'We Don't Run' is spray-painted on the bar wall?"

He nodded. "I came across an abandoned bar and tried to build a life off that. I called it The Hard Road because that is the story of my life, Arden. The path I've always taken...until now."

The next morning, Arden had one full day to enjoy before camp started. Arden's stomach rolled over with guilt at the thought of leaving Ross for a few weeks. Maybe her stomach was also upset for kissing Myth with Ross down the hallway. One thing Arden could smile about was knowing she would see Ross again in The Sky. But Mythias...she would probably never see him again. After camp, she will go back home and will not be able to visit Earth. She promised her uncle that she would never disobey him. She planned to keep her word. There would be too much at stake to go against Adao once more. Her fun, unpredictable days would be over. Mythias would grow older and live a life without her in it. Not even her shadow will be around him to witness his life. Palpable pain throbbed throughout her, she had to distance herself from those thoughts. She hardened herself and closed her thoughts off as if tying string to cut off one's circulation. She showered, put on fresh clothes, and visited Ross.

He looked sweaty but the green was fading. He encouraged her to experience camp, albeit with a scowl on his face. When she asked if her leaving upset him, he laughed it off. "You can do what you want, Arden. I'm not your king." He spat the words out as he switched positions in the bed. He sighed loudly and finally confided that he missed his family and wanted to get back to work. "A stagnant warrior is a dangerous one," he said. "Time to reflect isn't wise. I hate missing my work. I'm much needed these days." She listened to his frustrations and patted his hand as he complained.

Hours later, Arden made her way to the bar and saw a handsome figure sitting at the table, looking off into the distance. Distracted by her entrance, he quickly turned to look at her. No smile or friendliness in his face. *The men in this house were big-time downers.*

"You okay?" she asked aloud. He nodded his head. "You regret last night." She stated that instead of asking. He shook his head from side to side. She was not convinced. "Look, I can leave early—"

"I need to take a walk. I need some air. You up for that?" Arden's face relaxed and accepted the invite.

After drinking the last of coffee-cola, they went out on the front porch. It was a rainy day with a strong, slightly chilly breeze. She looked around the street and noticed the rich history there. Older homes were lined up and stood proudly. These houses have seen a lot and sheltered many. The cobblestone street as old and rough but beautiful in some way. She took a mental picture and realized this area held a special place in her heart that she will tell her kids about one day. When she was little, her mother would tell her stories about Earth and its people, make-believe fairy stories that sparked her imagination as a child. But one story her mother told her was *not* about Earth, but about a beautiful Sky Walker girl who died hundreds of years ago. She represented peace and lived in a grand white castle made of fluffy clouds and candy. She later ruled the cloud world and its people. Arden and all her friends dressed up as her at tea parties. They called her Queen Araline.

"Let's go," Myth stated.

Arden followed his lead as they made their way down the road with light rain sprinkling from above. He pointed out different houses, saying things like, "That's my friend Daniel's house." They came upon a park where the trees were plenty and the grass was bright green. This made her smile. They leaned against a sturdy tree and chatted about her education and how much she loves and misses the justice system. It was a perfect place to chat with its clear stream flowing close by and the grass was soft as a pillow. She laid down on the ground and stared at The Sky, her home. She watched as the sun shined brightly for only seconds. Myth was too distracted to notice. She stood up and joined Myth on a white park bench. Facing each other, she asked him a few questions, "Myth, why are you taking me on this walk?"

He looked down at his hands. "I'm angry at myself and needed air. I let myself get caught up last night and told you too much. I can't believe I explained the underground operation to Adao's niece who could easily go running to him about this information. Just not smart on my end. Please don't take offence, but I don't really know you." He stopped and looked at a passerby. "I've worked so hard to get a normal life—"

She quickly interjected, "I will not tell him. I would not do that to you. Plus, you said you stopped the operation so it's all fine."

He rolled his eyes rolled and scuffed. "Last night was not supposed to happen."

Arden's eyebrows rose. "Really? I thought you liked me. I thought you trusted me. Perhaps you humans kiss just anybody." She had more to say but words were leaving her head as if she had a gaping hole in her head.

"I can't like you, Arden. We are different. We are on different teams." He walked over to a nearby tree and leaned against it. "You will not survive in my world down here and I will *never* step foot in yours up there. You are not a human and I'm sure as hell not a Sky Walker." His words were thick with emotion. "Look, I'm trying to stay on the easy road. I am done taking the hard roads, Arden, and you sure as hell are a hard road. A winding, muddy, uphill, long, and hard road that I am not taking. Got it?"

Wow! His words shook her to the core as tears pooled in the corner of her eyes. "Fine, I get it! Even if we wanted to be together, we can't. But that does not mean you have to be bitter about what happened. Why can't we have that moment? Why ruin this day together?—I mean, you were my first kiss and I let myself be vulnerable with you." Standing up and joining him at the tree, she continued, "I can't help that

I like you." She took a deep breath and attempted to steady her shaking hands. "I mean, I understand your analogy, but don't be a fool, Mythias. You are *not* exactly a walk in the park either. You are a hard road to me too."

She was about to take off but he grabbed her arm and pulled her back. "Dammit, Arden! How do you want me to react? We. Can't. Do. This." He spoke each word slowly for emphasis. "As you can tell last night, I *want* to have this with you, but I can't. I'm allowed to be angry about it. You're just another thing that Adao is taking away from me now," he said between gritted teeth.

Her eyes narrowed and pushed him away but he yanked her closer. Then the world went silent. He kissed her so hard that she was nearly consumed with anger, desperation, and desire. She went limp into his arms and found herself kissing back intensely. She did not know how this would work but she had to try this hard road in her arms. Still kissing, she backed into the large tree and prayed it would keep her standing. His hands cupped her face as his lips began moving down her sensitive neckline. She wanted more…

"Excuse me!" came a voice that shattered like glass on a floor. They both pulled away quickly. Arden pushed the hair from out of her face and realized that they were kissing in public. A girl stood before them with her arms crossed and disdain plain to see on her made-up face.

He adjusted his shirt and looked at Arden. "Arden, I believe you know your soon-to-be camp advisor, Tess."

Arden and Spitter sputtered in unison, "You've got to be kidding me!"

Chapter 10

THE JOURNEY BACK to the bar was quiet and pensive. Mythias revealed that Tess was not only Arden's camp counselor, she was running the whole camp. Arden will admit that she did not act like a mature Sky Walker a few moments ago when she basically interrogated Tess as if she was a guilty defendant in the Sky Court. "Why on Earth would you be a camp advisor at a Sky Walker camp when you *hate* us?"

Tess didn't speak at first, but finally responded, "Because I needed a job and jobs are hard to find these days." Then she added, "Plus, Miss Fortunate, I have a family to take care of, unlike you. And I don't hate all Sky Walkers, I just hate *you*. Let's get that straight." Tess straightened her posture as she held her human nose up in the air.

Arden noticed that Tess' black hair was somehow even darker, perhaps an onyx color. Arden surmised it matched the color of her soul. "Why do you hate me when I've done nothing to you?"

Tess took a step closer and peered down at Arden. "I could tell a mile away by your superior stare that you thought you were better than me. You couldn't stop staring at me so I showed you a nice humanly gesture." She smiled showing brilliantly white teeth.

Arden did not let up. She stepped forward too. "You got the wrong idea. I was just nervous coming down here, and I do not think that way."

Tess laughed aloud. "You think you're royalty or something! You're just another overprivileged Sky Walker."

Arden smiled brightly. She wanted to hit her where it hurt. "Niece, actually, but considered a daughter. I am the daughter to King Oswin."

Tess' brown eyes widened as she tried to comprehend. She looked over at Mythias for confirmation. He nodded but kept his eyes on the ground. "Thought you were smarter than this!…Whatever! Just stay out of my way and we will be fine."

Is it playing the royalty card if Tess is the one who threw it down? That interaction felt icky to Arden. Tess grabbed Mythias to speak to him in private. She truly hoped that Myth didn't notice just how beautiful and strong Tess was, that he dismissed her perfect pale pink lips that complimented her beautiful shoulder-length, dark hair. Tess was a twisted puzzle that Arden did not feel like figuring out. As much as Arden disliked her, she would be blind if she did not notice that Tess was full of fire and beauty, much like a beloved phoenix.

Later, Myth came home to the bar, closed the door, and then leaned back against it. He spoke aloud to that he would be there for Arden and that he truly cared for her. He didn't want her to leave. His callused hands took hold of hers. "Are you okay?" he whispered into her ear.

Arden closed her eyes tightly and took in the warmth of him. After a few seconds, she grabbed his hand gently, led him to the back room, and shut the door. "Please just be with me. You don't have to kiss me or even say anything. Just be with me." His face softened. They both crawled to his bed and cuddled. He held her tight almost as if he hoped that all her worries would melt away.

Bam! The bedroom door went flying open. Arden and Myth startled awake to a very angry Ross. He was lying on the floor and pulling himself with his only good arm and his good leg. His coloring was purple and his face contorted.

"You! Back away from her!" he demanded in a warrior tone. He dragged himself further into the room.

She noticed that he had a nummer in his bad hand. "Ross, stop! You are not well—" she began but he the look on his face stopped her.

"You are a traitor, Arden! A traitor! You think I haven't figured you two out? Look at you, lying in bed together. It is wrong! You think that words do not penetrate these very walls? I know what you have been doing and I am appalled! He is a *human*! I cannot stand it any longer. I'm going mad!"

Arden's eyes filled with tears as she knelt down on the ground to assist him. "Call Dr. Koy! Hurry!" she yelled to Myth who got a running start, leaping over their heads to get to his phone in the other room. He was on a mission. "Ross, it's not what you think. We were just resting."

Ross sat down and then smacked Arden across the face with his good hand. Sweat beaded up on him and fell quickly to the ground. "Spare me! You are supposed to be different, Arden. You are a Kress! But you are a disgrace. You act innocent but you are not. I realized that in the time I have been *trapped* here. Not only am I disgusted by this, but I am also heartbroken. I mean…I thought you cared about me? You know we make sense, but you chose our sworn enemy. You are *literally* sleeping with the enemy!" He scoffed at her.

Guilt suddenly crushed her heart as much as his hand did to her face. "I'm going to speak slowly to you. I'm going to *try* to ignore…what you just did to me. I do care for you, Ross. Just let me help you up."

Arden went to help him. That was the last thing she remembered.

*****

Something was beeping in the distance. Arden's heart began to race. She was half asleep in a limbo of a horrible dream. She waded in the water and tried to resurface. "Wake up!" she told herself. She was numb. Echoes of voices were swirled above her as if on a static radio. The more she tried to tune in, the clearer the words became. She recognized Myth and Dr. Koy's voices, but there was a third voice. *Who was this third person? Why can't I wake up and move my body?*

"I still can't believe this! It's a wonder she's even alive!" Koy said.

There was shuffling noises. She realized that the third person was male, which stumped her. She did not know this person's voice. It was not Ross. "Arden, if you can hear me, this will only hurt for a few seconds."

He was not joking. Invisible screams seared through her inside her head as it finally brought her back to consciousness. Then she made a real scream and opened her eyes. She found her right arm was fully bandaged, and her head was throbbing. She sat straight up and immediately became dizzy.

"Easy, Arden! It's Koy."

She focused on his vivid green eyes and realized she was now fully awake. Relief flooded her body, forgetting the pain momentarily. Her eyes swept the room to take in everything. It was too bright for her vulnerable eyes. She looked around for Ross. *Where was Ross?* Mythias was holding her hand, worry heavy on his face. She then moved her head to see the third person, which turned out to be Fletcher. "Fletcher! I'm happy you are here…but why are you here?"

"You know I work the post around the corner. I happened to be walking by when I heard a commotion here at The Hard Road so I came to help. Then I saw Ross, my fellow warrior, and you. I was surprised, to say the least."

Arden blushed lightly. "Please don't tell on me. Myth is the friend I told you I was staying with."

Fletcher eyed Arden then sized up Mythias. "Why would I do that? You have dirt on me, after all," he joked. He had a way of making her feel better. Her heart felt lighter. "What I am confused about though, Arden, is maybe you can tell me why Ross tried to kill you…and why this human guy has been glued to you this whole time?"

Myth dropped Arden's hand and stared Fletcher down in a way that would make even a warrior cower. Arden decided not to address it yet and said she would fill him in later. She looked down at her injured arm, which was burned severely. Koy had given her aloe-healer in hopes that she would take to it better than Ross did. Koy explained everything that happened. Ross used the nummer on Arden's arm, causing burns and deep cuts. Then he proceeded to hit her in the head with the handle, hence the blackout. When Arden asked how he was doing and where he was, Koy stated that they moved Ross to his house so he could keep an eye on him more. He suggested it was probably wise to keep Ross separate from Arden and Myth for the time being. Turned out he had a severe fever and was belligerent.

"Ross doesn't remember this altercation but he feels absolutely horrible about hurting you. There are no words to describe his guilt."

Part of her was relieved that he was okay but another part wanted to kick him in the neck—hard. She knew deep down though that Ross would never hurt her in his normal mind, even though he is a Striker. She was certain of it. She decided that once fully healed, she would visit him and *maybe* try mending their friendship, but she needed to mend herself first. Koy stood up and motioned for everyone to leave. "Wait!" Her yell echoed throughout the place. "I can still go to camp, right?"

Koy played with his chin hair and thought for a moment. He explained that perhaps she could go but she would have to wait some days to really give the aloe time to do its job. If she responds poorly to the aloe-healer, then she would have to stay here. She kept her hopes high anyway. All this talking and thinking was making her head spin. She lay down to rest her soul, body, and mind.

*****

Arden awoke from her deep slumber days later. She stretched out her sore body and called out to Myth to ask for some water. She sounded like a croaking frog. She winced at her arm almost as if she forgot it was harmed. He came in with a cold glass and a blank face. His hair was messy and he had dark circles under his eyes. She missed that face tremendously and was hoping for a big smile. No such luck with this guy. His vibe and aurora were all wrong and she sensed it. "I think I'm doing better. My head is not throbbing and I feel more…normal. Let's take a look at the damage, shall we?" she announced. Her voice was still hoarse and deep, which reminded her of a good friend back home by the name of Arkin. He always had a raspy voice. She smirked and adjusted her weakened torso upright on the bed.

Myth seemed reluctant. "How about we wait for Koy."

She did not like that answer. She muttered under her breath something about him being a baby and started to unwrap her arm in defiance. As she unraveled the bandage bit by bit, she became more and more worried as her eyebrows scrunched together. The aloe-healer has been working so nicely on her so she did not know what she was so anxious about. Something felt off. She eventually removed the aloe wrap. As the dressing hit the ground, her eyes were glued to her unidentifiable arm. This was not her arm. *What the hell is this thing?* She was looking at a sorry excuse for an appendage. The skin was bright pink and severely wilted. The burnt area now had a gigantic scar up and down her entire arm. She also realized that there were scars on her shoulder, neck, and part of her leg. The damaged skin looked red and shriveled and oozing liquid nonstop. Her breath was caught in her throat. It felt like a snake's useless dead skin. She sat in silence and close her eyes once more, right before she screamed her head off.

*****

With her bag packed, Koy made sure she had some aloe-healer to go with her since she was on the last stages of the healing process. Arden looked down at her arm and shook her head in despair. How was she going to explain this to her family? She would have to come up with a creative story. She could not believe that she would be forever scarred like this. She knew Ross did not mean to cause her harm, but that did not mean that it still didn't affect her. That gruesome scar will forever be a reminder to be careful around friends, even someone you love. No matter who it is, you may be burned.

"You ready to finally get to camp tomorrow morning?" Myth asked curiously.

It was just Arden and Myth at The Hard Road. She loved the freedom with that. In a selfish way, she rejoiced that Ross was not down the hall. No one who could overhear or judge them. It was the last night she would be with Myth. This night meant everything. Once she went to camp in the morning, no more Mythias. She shivered at the thought of losing him. She kept forgetting that she was the hard road that he did not want to travel. She bit her bottom lip and looked up at Myth. He was the perfect height for her. "You know I am a little excited, but I'm tempted to skip it and stay here with you."

He shook his head after hearing her words. "Nope, you're going."

With her eyebrows furrowed, dhe crossed her arms and lifted her chin high. "Why can't I stay here with you for the next few weeks? We would have a lot of fun together. There's so much I don't know yet about you."

Myth gave a sardonic laugh. "After what you have gone through just to get to that camp? You're not giving up this learning opportunity, especially for me. I'm temporary, Arden."

She sighed dramatically. "But you can show me things. Let me fully experience Earth with you. You can be my learning opportunity." Myth stood up and stretched his arms. He turned his back to her and said no in a low tone. Arden stood up and crept behind him. "Please stop saying that. I really do not want to go to camp now. Plus, everyone is already settled in. I would be considered new at this point. I have a little over a week to stay down here. You are all I want to see and experience. I yearn to understand you more. I think you know what that would entail."

Myth turned to face her with a look of torture. She could tell he was truly thinking about it. Maybe her eloquence could penetrate his broody barriers. "Look, you staying will make everything harder and more complicated for both of us. You *need* to go. If you stay longer, then I don't know what I will do to you. You think that kiss was something, you have no idea the lengths I would take you. That cannot *and* will not happen." He touched her milky face and looked her dead in the eye. "Please…for me… don't ask again." He closed his eyes tightly shut.

She felt his pain, but it made it worse. Arden grabbed a seat at her favorite table. "This is our last night together then." Tears fell down her face and down onto the wooden table. She could not hold it in. It did not matter at this point anyway. Everything felt so…absolute. She was not sure if what she felt was love but she did know that it was real and deep. "Maybe if we give this some time, we can figure something out. Some kind of a loophole on seeing each other. It would be super hard but we could try. I'm willing to try anything." She sat up and looked at him expectantly.

He was teary-eyed and quiet. He slumped down next to her, his graceful face full of stubble. "Arden, sweetie, I can't do *super hard*, you know this. It's not in me." He swallowed and continued calmly, "You deserve a beautiful life in The Sky. I bet it is an amazing world up there. You need a Sky Walker to share a life with. Hell, you're royalty up there. We have nothing in common, really. You cannot love me. I'm just…a human."

She shuddered. That last sentence was all she could handle. She felt a totally new sort of pain. The realization that this was indeed a lost cause felt soul-shattering. Her hand touched his as he wiped the tears from his eyes. She ran back to his bedroom and slammed the door. Her world was crashing. She took several deep breaths and forced herself to stop crying. She was dying inside. She looked around the room one last time. The memories would be forever in her mind and heart. Her fingers snatched up the smallest patch from his collection. She needed something to remember him by. The bed was calling her name. She took deep breaths and buried her face deep into the soft pillow. She would never forget this smell, the essence of Mythias. The man she could never have. Her wobbly legs found the ground and she stood up unsteady. After another brief scan, she saw his dirty white shirt that she wore some time ago. She placed in her bag for safekeeping. She was a thief, yes. She stole his shirt and patch, but he stole her heart so now they were even. Sort of…not really.

Chapter 11

ARDEN WALKED BACK through the bar area with her belongings in tow. She automatically searched for Mythias, but he wasn't there. She called out his name to a silent room. No response. Her bare feet walked around one last time and decided to make her exit. She silently said good-bye to his home as she lightly touched the large table. Placing the patch against her heart, she walked out of The Hard Road to the moonlit city outside. With the camp paperwork in her hand, she started on her short journey. Judging by the map on her paperwork, she would arrive there in no time. Echoes filled the night air as she walked briskly on the gravel path. Passing The Landing, she noticed the post that Fletcher worked at was empty. Begrudgingly, she used her domed band and asked it for help. She hated using her dome because it became a crutch to many. She wanted to use her instincts, but at this point…"Screw it!" she said out loud. The dome read the map and spoke the directions aloud. She was much closer than she thought.

After twenty minutes of walking, Arden saw a large camping area in the distance. A tall brick building stood among smaller buildings. Trees were abundant, making it look idyllic in the dim light. It was just as beautiful at night as in the day. A huge body of water sparkled and looked much cleaner than the other lakes she had seen on Earth. Butterflies fluttered in her stomach and she felt like vomiting for a second. Her hand went up to her mouth and she bent over just in case. She felt dizzy and her arm was starting to twitch in pain. It was time for her aloe-healer, she realized. Cracking her neck back and forth, she straightened up and pushed through her discomfort. Her bare feet shuffled again toward the huge campsite. Walking down a hill, she approached a building gate. It was closed at this time and no one was around. The sign on the gate read, "Ivy Grove." Seeing her middle name made her stop and smile. It was *fate*! She tried to open the gate but it was locked tight. She made her way back to a small shelter house and laid down on the ground, deciding to get some sleep. With her bag serving as a pillow, she was getting quite cozy and soon drifted off to sleep.

A short while later, she heard her name in the distance, telling her to wake up. When she opened her eyes, it was still dark. Suddenly, a form stood over her. She jumped up and retreated before she realized that it was her good friend, Ellery. A smile spread on Arden's stunned face.

Ellery lounged in for a big hug and kiss. "I thought you'd never come! I nearly stepped on you! What the heck are you doing down there, anyway?" Her eyes were wide and her hands expressive.

Arden became defensive. "I couldn't get in. Think I was sleeping out here for my own good?" Arden hugged her friend again. "What are you doing out at this hour anyway?"

Ellery jumped up and down in a girly way and clapped her hands. "It's a secret, actually, so don't say anything. No one else knows this, but there is a guy that I really like. Well, we are supposed to meet by the white oak tree up the hill there." She pointed her talon up to where Arden had just come from.

"*Wow!* Who is it?" This was news to Arden because they never talked about boys except Ravel Reed.

Ellery looked around to make sure no one was around. "His name is Arkin, he is a little older. He is a writer and really cute."

Arden was happy for her dear friend and realized that she wanted to talk about the man she likes but stopped herself. "I know Arkin. He has the deep, raspy voice. You are right, he is handsome. I am happy for you. So how's camp so far?" she asked.

"It's been great! I have a feeling you will really like our forestry and writing class. I will guide you tomorrow where to go. There are many options. Anyway, I better go see Arkin before he misses me! Oh, wait…here is my badge. It will let you in. It has my room name and letter on it. Just sleep in my room tonight. See you!" Ellery sprinted off into the misty night of love.

Arden rolled her eyes and grinned. She used the borrowed badge and walked into the campgrounds. It was a dirty but beautiful place, very rustic and homey. She saw the capital *F* on the badge so she walked to the building with the corresponding letter on the front door and opened it. She snuck down the hall and looked around. A big, cozy lounge room had a floor-to-ceiling stone fireplace and books everywhere—human books. She remembered *Vintage Lovely* and felt she would not be opening that book for a long time. Her heartache was very raw and hurt much like her arm. After taking in the scenery, she really needed to lie down, put medicine on it, and get some sleep. She found the door that read "Pish Posh," indicating that it was indeed Ellery's room. There was a scanner on the side of the door that read the badge then unlocked. She swung the wooden door open and looked around. She expected someone else to be sleeping in her room, bunk beds or something. She sighed in relief. She liked the thought of the solidarity that the room provided. She quickly applied some aloe-healer to her aching skin. Throwing the bag on the floor, she quickly jumped in bed, dirty feet and all. It felt damn good. She sprawled out and was out faster than you can say Mythias.

*****

The morning sun slowly peeked in through the only window in Ellery's room. With sunlight on her face, she yawned and stretched her legs in bed. Ellery wasn't back yet. She proceeded to take a shower to remove yesterday's muck and then wait for Ellery to return. Arden did not want to leave without Ellery but it was 9:00 a.m. so she ventured out on her own. She did not like codependence anyway. Strolling down halls, she picked up the aroma of bread coming from another building. She quickly went in to find a big cafeteria full of people eating breakfast and chatting. She grabbed her chest when she noticed Dekker sitting in the back of the room eating.

He caught her eye and ran up to her as if he had not seen her in ten years. He scooped her up in a hug and twirled her around. Setting her back on her feet, he leaned down and kissed her cheek. "I thought you were dead or something. Where have you been?"

She smiled sheepishly. "That story will be told later. Right now, I need *food*!"

He escorted her to her favorite birdseed, oats, and fruit. Then she sat down with him and some other familiar faces, gobbling down food. She had to admit that she missed her friends. After eating, Dekker showed Arden to the Welcoming Lobby to check in. It had a cathedral ceiling with stained glass above a marble floor, which resembled something from The Sky. If she would had worn shoes, it would definitely echo in this grand place. An enormous dark wooden desk stood proudly in the middle of the room and piles of paper were stacked on the floor nearly to ceiling. White glossy folders with large numbers on them were hanging from wires in an extremely sophisticated pulley system for them to move around.

"Next!" shouted a high-pitched voice. A bright face emerged from the top of the desk. "Hi there, I'm Bianca. I will be taking care of you today!" The blonde-haired, blue-eyed human who looked about Arden's age gave her a room key that read *G* for the room named "Hopscotch." "Name please?" The human beamed at Arden.

"Arden Ivy Kress." Arden's eyes squinted as she tried to understand that word. She had no idea what *hopscotch* was.

"A food, perhaps? Like butterscotch?" Arden questioned aloud.

Bianca giggled in high octaves and then proceeded to correct her. "*Um*...it's a hopping game, actually. Super, super, super fun! You go *hop*, *hop*, *hop*. You will learn about it, Miss Sky Walker Friend." Bianca's energy was palpable. She smiled so wide, it looked like it hurt. "There's a Human Basics class if you are interested." Arden liked this human, she was comforting. She wondered if she could stay with Bianca for the rest of the trip as her own personal peppy tour guide. Bianca asked Arden to sign some papers as she maneuvered the pulley ropes in different directions to get a folder from the air. Blowing the hair from her face, she sat down on a chair. "All set, Miss Kress. I most certainly hope you enjoy your time here. Good day!"

Arden came upon a huge sign that read, "Available Classes: Forestry, Writing, Cooking, History, Medicine, Sports, and Mysteries." Her mind kept going to cooking for some reason. It was probably because of how fascinating it was to watch Mythias cook and have passion for it. She did not have to rush this learning thing though. Everyone could make their own schedule and attend the classes they wanted. Arden took a deep breath as she watched humans and Sky Walkers having conversations in the halls together. Hugging a human book she picked up from the Bianca's desk, she closed her eyes and soaked it all in. It was the beginning of another adventure.

Arden walked slowly and visited all the buildings on site, enjoying the outdoors. Then she found an empty bench outside the main check-in hall. But instead of sitting, she laid her body out on the entire length of it. The sunshine was dancing on her face as the smell of pine trees permeated the air. The sound of distant laughter floated in the breeze. She thought she could even hear Bianca's singing voice in the distance. She gave a little prayer to God and let him know how much she appreciated him for this opportunity. Complete bliss filled her soul. For a moment, the haunting thoughts of Mythias and Ross seemed to drift off.

All of a sudden, she heard someone approaching her, heralded by the snapping of branches. As she listened intently, she tried to be nonchalant. When the sound stopped abruptly, an odd feeling came over her. She opened one eye. A shaky Sky Walker stood before her, barely standing. A girl covered in blood from head to toe with gory cuts on her face and body. She tried to speak but fear had taken the girl's voice away as she trembled severely. Arden's eyes widened in horror when she recognized her friend, Ellery Persephone Stosik.

Chapter 12

ARDEN'S LEGS MOVED faster than ever. She jumped up and grabbed Ellery's cold body just as she collapsed on the ground. She was deadweight in Arden's arms. Fear gripped Arden. "Help!" she then screamed it from the top of her lungs. Her voice hit optics that she never knew existed. "Help!" Her bloodied friend was near death and she was in sheer panic. Everything moved in slow motion as Arden examined Ellery's beautiful, lifeless face. Carrying her friend like a wounded soldier from battle, Arden began running for help with renewed strength. She crashed through the front door of the Welcoming Lobby. The noise echoed throughout the halls, causing people to stop in their tracks. "Help! Please!" She laid her best friend on a bench inside. "Please help her!" Arden fell to her knees and placed her head down on Ellery's stomach. "You will not die!" She screamed at Ellery.

Out of nowhere, arms wrapped around Arden and guided her to a wooden chair. People were hovering over Ellery and working quickly on her. Unexpectedly, a strong yet calm voice came from the overhead. "Emergency, Welcoming Lobby!" Only a few seconds went by when a rush of men and women in white coats came storming toward them. They must had been doctors working in the medical teaching area. They were speaking gibberish that Arden assumed were medical words. They picked Ellery up and put on a moving white bed with wheels. The blood quickly soaked into the sheets. The last thing Arden saw was Ellery's dirty feet as they wheeled her friend away. Arden could not move. She just sat there trying to breathe and comprehend what just happened to her friend. Her energetic, free-spirited, wholesome, and beautiful friend.

Dekker suddenly appeared, pulling Arden out of her shocked reverie. He shook Arden to bring her back to reality. "What happened?"

"I don't know. I was just lying on a bench when she came up in a bloody mess. I carried her in here for help. What could have possibly happened to her?"

Dekker shook his head and had tears glistening on his face. They were confused. "Maybe she was in class and got hurt?" he said aloud.

"No, she wasn't in class…" Arden trailed off when she realized where Ellery had spent her night. "Arkin!" she exclaimed as if she found the answer to this puzzle.

"Wait, what?" Dekker asked, frowning.

"She was with Arkin all night! He must know something!"

She would tie him up Striker-style and lock him up in High Rise, if she had to. They walked throughout the halls in search of him. Suddenly, it dawned on Arden that he could be anywhere. She marched up to Bianca working at the front desk. "I need your help. Please page Arkin Noble to the Welcoming Lobby immediately."

The girl studied Arden and became nervous. "Oh dear, oh dear, oh dear! Is there another issue? I just don't know how I will handle another—"

"Just do it!" Dekker snapped.

The PA system rang, "*Uh*, Arkin Noble, please come to the Welcoming Lobby immediately. Arkin Noble?"

They waited. After the longest five minutes in their existence had passed, Arden requested that he be paged again. Dekker and Arden walked around in circles. He did not come. Arden had enough of waiting and started running back to where she bumped into Ellery last night. She approached the big black gate and turned into the nondescript building. A man dressed in all blue was working at the gate. He eyed her as she approached him. "Just taking a look," she said to the blue man.

He gave a breathy laugh. "Why is that?" He seemed interested.

"Something happened to my friend. I'm going to figure it out. You know anything about an attack?"

His eyes darkened. "An attack here?"

This guy was wasting their precious time. Her view shifted to the outside trail of the hill she struggled with the night before. "She mentioned meeting him at an oak tree up the hill." Their bare feet were muddy tracking through the path.

"Do you know what an oak tree looks like?" Dekker asked with apprehension.

Arden nodded. They approached the abnormally large tree that stood out like a human in the clear blue Sky. It did not really belong there. The Earth was singing its natural lullaby as they caught their breath from the strenuous hill. Dekker was quiet as he slowly walked around the tree and its wooded surroundings, looking for any sign of a struggle. Arden did the same thing. They did not speak to each other until twenty minutes later when they sat down on a large mossy log to rest. Their knees were touching as they held hands. She needed his closeness and support.

"We have to figure this out," she announced. "How is there not a trace of her blood or any sign of an attack? How is that possible, Dekker?"

He shook his head. "Maybe she didn't stay at this tree all night. Maybe she met Arkin and then they went to a place to spend the night?"

All they could do was look at each other. Arden swallowed hard and asked the question they didn't want to face. "What if she dies?"

"You must have hope, Arden. Have faith in the doctors' hands. Have faith in the warriors who will track and investigate. Have faith in King Adao for no one hurts his people. Ultimately, have faith in Ellery."

She nodded in affirmation and then said aloud, "Ellery seems weak, but she's one of the strongest I know. Others see a small, happy, and free person. Often they have mistaken her kindness for weakness. She is not weak. Quiet strength…that is the definition of my Ellery."

When Dekker and Arden returned, they were told that Ellery was sent to a hospital and will be transferred home in The Sky as soon as she's able. She was not allowed a visitor of any kind. Arden already tried arguing her way through that but was denied. Even the royalty card didn't work!

Strict orders from King Adao. After an exhausting day, she parted ways with Dekker who was in the *B* building in a room named “Seesaw.” Her tired mind luckily remembered her building and room name. She entered her room, unpacked her belongings, and slept for several hours.

When morning came, Arden realized that her first day at camp was unforgettable and surprising. As bad as the Ellery situation was, at least she did not have time to pine for Mythias. He felt like a dream…almost not as real anymore, although the pain in her heart still stung. Eyeing her bag, she was tempted to pack her belongings back up and head for The Sky, her beautiful and comfortable home. A place where one can breathe and not get odd looks. A perfect place where there were zero Spitters—*Tess!* She completely forgot about the dark soul who was running this camp. That was her mission today, speak with Tess and try to get updates on Ellery and Mythias. She was the main camp leader. She had to be full of information. She skipped breakfast and made her way to find Tess. Luckily, she spotted Bianca and waved at her. Bianca smiled brightly and scurried over to Arden to see what she needed. Her ponytail was high on her head and she was always impeccably dressed. She wore pastels and reminded Arden of sweet, freshly whipped cotton candy with long blonde hair down to her bottom.

“Can you please tell me where to find Tess?”

An unpleasant facial expression crossed her face. That was the face of someone who stumbled across the wrath of said dark soul. This made Arden giggle slightly then felt guilty immediately. Bianca said, “Yes, I know her. She’s in the gym area where the sports classes are held. That's her favorite hangout, which is totally fine with me. The gym is the furthest building from my working station." Bianca winked at Arden and took off skipping in the other direction.

Arden could not help but be amused. She turned on her heel in search of this mystery gym. Walking outside, she looked for the furthest building from Bianca. Lo and behold, she found it. The heavy door squeaked open and closed abruptly behind her as bright lights invaded her eyes. There were dirty red-and-blue mats stacked on the floor along the walls. Circular bouncing things were resting on a shiny metal rack. Tables of different sizes and nets were placed throughout the huge domed room. Whistles were echoing loudly. People yelling and cheering other people on. Excitement filled the air. It reminded her of the Flying Festival, the only thing she could compare it to. She noticed Sky Walkers were playing an unfamiliar game wearing odd clothing that had numbers on the back of their shirts. Musky sweat lingered in the air as she passed by, trying to go unnoticed. This was not her scene. She did not want to play. She was strictly here for business. Tess' tall form stood in the distance as she was pointing at things and telling others what to do. Arden walked up to her.

"Hello, how are you?" Arden said with an unsure smile.

Tess looked up at her. "*Ah*, you do exist. I've been looking for you."

"Really?

"Yes, I have news. She's going to be fine. She is alive and due to go back to The Sky after some medical attention. So she's a good friend of yours?"

Relief filled Arden. "Yes, what happened to her?"

Tess shrugged her shoulders. "Seems we don't have answers yet, however, your grand old uncle said he will find out the story and there will be repercussions for my camp." Tess' face became nervous. There was panic in those glassy eyes. "What if I lose my job? What if he closes down the camp?" Tess' hands covered her face.

Arden rested her hand on Tess' shoulder and said, "I won't let that happen. I promise." Tess removed her hands, revealing big eyes that closed in relief. Arden could feel the worry in her face. "So look, I was wondering if we could maybe hang out some?" Arden asked.

Tess started stretching her arms and legs, still keeping eye contact. "Interesting. Well, stay for a dance class and we can hang out after."

When Arden thought of dancing, she pictured the movements the Sky Walkers did at wedding ceremonies. "Is someone getting married or something?" She wondered aloud.

Tess burst out laughing. She looked like a completely different person. This was not Spitter because a happy Tess seemed impossible. "No, Arden, we don't do marriages down here anymore. That's a thing of the past. I'm talking about dancing for fun. You must stay."

Arden had a feeling she was going to regret it but decided to sign up anyway. A pleasant verbal exchange with Spitter called for a mini celebration.

Chapter 13

"ONE…TWO…THREE…FOUR…MOVE! FIVE… SIX…SEVEN…EIGHT…REPEAT! RELAX your shoulders!" Tess was barking orders to the few Sky Walkers who remorsefully signed up.

Arden thought the movements just did not make sense. *Hips were not meant to twist like that,* she thought. It felt wrong, but Arden was committed to get through the routine. Arden could not help her blushing face, feeling awkward and seductive at the same time. How was that even possible? The dance class ended up being educational as they learned some ancient ballroom moves, old hip-hop, and something modern she liked called "kinetics." When the class was over, she made sure to tell Tess that it was surprisingly fun and informative. She was glad she had stayed for it. She was even happier to later pry into the mind of Tess, Mythias' ex-girlfriend.

Glitter was floating in the air as Arden followed Tess down a dark hallway. Where did it even come from? Her body was sweaty, she tried fanning cool air toward her face. Her door was big and black with a yellow sign that read "Beehive." She looked over her shoulder to answer the unsaid question, "I'm busy. That's the way I like it." She opened the door and let Arden go in first. The walls were dark and covered in classy black-and-white landscape pictures that seemed to not exist down here in the human world anymore, breathtaking photos of a world that once was. "They were my grandmothers," she announced. It was a reserved room but had a few splashes of color throughout. The young ladies made their way to focal point of the room, a huge wooden coffee table. It was low to the ground and had about twenty big puffy cushions that surrounded the table in masses. Vibrant colors that were in contrast to her surroundings. Arden fell back onto the oversized cushions that felt more like clouds. As Tess went to grab some drinks, this was her moment to analyze her room. There were pictures of people on her walls. Happy pictures. Some art sculptures made of clay material were scattered around the place. A little girl who looked very familiar caught her eye. She had a big smile on her face and a glint in her eyes. "That's my little sister, Ivy," Tess stated as she entered the room.

Arden's mouth opened in surprise. "Ivy is your sister? I know her!"

Tess joined her on the cushions and handed her a glass with fizzy purple liquid in it. "Wait a minute, she told me about a Sky Walker who came to her rescue the other day in the market. That had to be you then?" she asked. Arden nodded her head and smiled. "I want to thank you. Ivy is my life...well, her and our father."

Arden pressed her lips together and thought hard. "Does he wear an eye patch?"

Tess' dark-haired head bobbed up and down. "They drum up business and get the paperwork started for my camp. Then I run the camp that I named after my Ivy."

Tess is normal and capable of being sappy. Who knew? Arden took a sip of the fizzy drink. "Ivy Grove Campgrounds. Is Grove your last name?"

Tess shifted and tucked her legs under her behind. She put her hair up in a high ponytail and then answered, "Grover, actually, but Ivy Grove makes more sense, you know."

Arden was confused. "No, I don't know. What does Ivy mean?"

Tess giggled some. "Why are you so interested?"

"Because Ivy is my middle name. I never really thought about what it meant. It is not a known name in The Sky. I'm the only one I know of that was named Ivy."

Tess explained that ivy is a type of plant that has heart-shaped leaves and climbs along walls on Earth. "It's resilient, really strong, and sometimes creepy." Tess thought that last part was hilarious. They both laughed in a hardy and girly manner.

"I can be creepy." Arden smiled and then became silent.

Tess elbowed her lightly. "Why are you acting so odd?"

After a few seconds had passed, she finally spoke up. "It's just that…since we don't have ivy up in The Sky, how did my mom know that name if she'd never been to Earth before? No one, not even my father, made it to Earth until that day they were killed. Where did they hear that from?" She gulped down the rest of her drink.

"Well, I'm sure there are other names that are used up in The Sky and down here too. Maybe it's not as odd as you think?" In that moment, Arden decided to let it go.

Hours passed by filled with random conversations. The topics ranged from dancing to old-timey marriages. Tess felt the need to keep the human ways intact. As she spoke of her kind, she kept her head held high. She remembered her mother and grandmother's stories about the past filled with beautiful weddings, all-you-can-eat buffets, electronic devices, and much more. There were love in people. Yes, there was hate too, but love was present, and it was beautiful. They talked about Tess' family and how she was the one providing for them. Her mother had been taken away from the Sky Walkers and she has been resentful ever since.

"I'm sorry she was taken away. I am sorry that our presence made many lives harder, but I promise you, this was not my father's intent. I hope it's not my uncle's either. My father was a great person. I cannot persuade you nor do I want to diminish your feelings in any way so I just want to say that I am sorry for our losses."

Tess looked up at Arden. She grabbed her hand and squeezed it. "Holy mother of pearl, look at your talons! This is a no-no." Tess disappeared for a moment into a bathroom and came back with a colorful box full of paints. She grabbed Arden's hands and began to file them down with a long abrasive file. Arden surrendered her nails and watched Tess' every move. "It's just an emery board, is all." After seeing Arden's face, she put the emery board down and offered to just paint them. Arden picked out clear polish with black tips. What she liked was that her talons were still very sharp but looked better.

More time passed. Arden found herself thinking of Mythias, which brought a raw ache deep in her chest. It was only be a few days but felt like it had been months since she was away from him. She took a deep breath. "S, I'm curious. I know we are not close, but are you open to some questions?"

Tess laid back on the cushions and blew on her wet nails. "I think so." Tess was staring up at the ceiling in anticipation.

"Mythias…I know you two were together. How long was your relationship and how did it happen?" Just the thought of them together made her insides shrivel.

"We were childhood friends. He was my first boyfriend and my last, honestly. We were on and off for years. You know how that goes with boys. Frankly, I just was not interested in other people. Mythias…he felt real. Plus, as you know, he's super cute."

"Tell me more. What happened?"

Tess rubbed her nose and rolled over to look at Arden. "We were too much alike. We were feeding off each other with our dark thoughts, our anger for Adao and what had happened to our parents. The very thing that brought us together was also pulling us apart. He is a very decent person but we are not meant to be with each other. Took me longer to figure out than it did him. He broke my heart and I broke his nose." She made a fist and wore a smirk.

Arden smiled reluctantly. "Do you miss him?" Tess shook her head no.

"I should be asking you that. Do you miss Mythias?" Tess asked Arden the same question.

Arden's throat threatened to close. She looked down at the ground and realized she hated feeling vulnerable. "Yes, I miss him. I will never see him again."

Tess sat up. "Arden, I know you miss him but I really don't see how this would work out. A human and a Sky Walker? It just would not work. I'm really sorry though. And just so you know, he can be very demanding…and moody. Consider yourself lucky to just move on before you fell in love."

Her honesty was riveting but her words were tiny jabs into her soul. Tears dropped from her blue eyes. "By living these experiences, I feel so privileged. To hurt as my heart does now is beautiful. What I have noticed from these experiences is that in The Sky, we are very safe. We do not feel the same things as you do down here. We do not feel the emotions as much. There are no dangers, no major struggles. Humans suffer, love wildly, know deep hunger, know excessive thirst, and feel real hatred and hurt, and work hard for very little money, not to mention having beings hovering above and waiting for you to make a mistake. That has to be stressful, now that I see it from your view and that is meant literally, too. In The Sky, yes, we may argue, but it is out of the love of law. We may be sad but it is over frivolous things. We love, but it is an organized love, not the humanly love. Everything is structured and fits inside law book that King Adao had written. Even though my people watch you humans every day, we know so little about you all. Sorry, my emotions and insights have grown tremendously. I do not know how to deal with it. I've been so poorly equipped for such situations."

Tess grabbed Arden's hand and sat down right next to her. "What you haven't seen yet is a human friendship that can move mountains and make the darkest of nights bright. I can't believe I like you, but I do, Bird Girl. I'm here for you and think that us coming together was for a reason. Something big, it feels."

She got out tons of different dresses, leather outfits, and her bold makeup cases. The honey mead was flowing freely while the two were singing and trying on different outfits. Arden's favorite outfit that she kept on was a white tank top, black leather skirt, dark green combat boots, and black stockings. Tess styled Arden's hair in long straight pieces with strands of army-green hair popped out in places. Her makeup was not too wild but a lot of mascara and eyeliner were applied for the smokiest eyes ever. They started to settle down quickly. In full human attire, Arden was sprawled out on the floor chewing gum for the first time that Tess made naturally from a sweet gum tree at camp. Tess told Arden about a dance during the last night of camp and how fun it was, a memorable way to end camp. Every female would wear a nice evening gown and the males dress up in jacket-and-trouser attire. Tess said she would let Arden pick her dress before anyone else can.

At this point, Arden was thankful but past being tipsy and really yearning for her bed. She stood up and said her good night to Tess. Arden let herself out the big door, shut it softly behind her, and waited for the click. She rubbed her face hard and stretched her arms above her, the scarred arm was still a bit tender. She started to walk down the hallway when she had heard something fall to the right. She pivoted in anticipation. Slowly moving her feet in front of another, she realized that combat boots were much louder than her bare feet. She heard a running noise. She made her way past a dimly lit kitchen with black-and-white checkered floors. She pulled back the soft curtain on a framed white window was in front of her and peered out. Nothing. Just foreign trees blowing in the wind. She moved into the kitchen and decided that she was no longer interested in this little pursuit. Emotions and mead had too strong of a hold of her. She turned on her feet and went out the main entrance. The shadowy night welcomed her as she started toward for her building. Standing outside was sublime to her senses. The cool air sent chills down her spine. Watching the constellations gleam brightly above, she realized she missed reading books on the stars and planets. The gloriously complex solar system was something they studied when she was younger, but Adao restricted it once he became king. He felt that such talk was aligned with the "cloud books," making it useless.

Stumbling out of her reverie, she was about to open the door to her building when, without warning, she heard a clamor behind her. She turned around quickly, her stance aggressive and waiting. She looked down to see a little animal tied up to a tree close by, an animal she has never seen before. It was furry, jumpy, and adorable. She walked to it in hesitation, but this animal seemed welcoming and excited to see her. She kneeled onto her knees and cautiously extended her scarred hand out to this bouncing thing. It rolled over onto its back and made sweet whimpering squeaks. She began to rub its belly and it squirmed in the most delightful of ways. This made her laugh aloud. "What on Earth are you? I'm Arden and I'm from The Sky." She hated to see the poor thing tied up so she took him to her room, holding him tight. "You are just too precious!" She was baby talking for the first time in her life to an unidentified animal. "I'll take care of you. However, you probably belong to someone. *Hmm!*" She spoke aloud as if he understood her. "I will put you back outside tomorrow morning and wait for your owner. If they do not come, then I shall keep you forever. How does that sound?" she argued to herself.

As she made her way to her room (Hopscotch), she noticed her door was already slightly open. Her cautious hands slowly pushed open the door where she froze like a statue and nearly dropped her new friend to the floor. She was not expecting company at this time at night, especially in her bedroom and especially not *him*. He stood tall before her and immediately approached her with an eager presence. His hands found her face and kissed her with all his might. Something moved deep down inside her, but she mustered strength to pull herself away. She caught her breath as he fell down to one knee. His hands were in begging position, his face stained with tears. He was a little unsteady now. She was speechless for a moment before she finally muttered one breathy word, "Ross."

Chapter 14

THE AZURE SKY was bright as several Sky Walkers were hovering above. Phoenixes blow ferocious fire into the air almost as a threat to those below. She realized that it must be exasperating for humans to be watched and judged daily.

Arden was lying on a thick blanket on the muddy grass, letting her mind float away on a cloud. Her current dark thoughts were lifted out into the unknown. She thought of it as a type of "spring cleaning" in her own way, a cleansing of the mind. She'd love to forget Myth's piercing eyes and everything else about him. Somehow, someway she wanted to make room for some beautiful memories of Earth that did not revolve around Myth or drama. Even the cooking class she took reminded her too much of him. She did learn, however, how to make a grilled cheese sandwich and tomato soup. This food combo could possibly be the best thing on Earth. She smiled to herself thinking of the hot goodness. Her black-painted talons were starting to chip a little, she noticed, as she laid there loving the quiet Earth.

"Can we talk?" came Ross' voice, pulling her from her daydream.

She sighed and propped herself up on her elbows to look at him. She swept her hair back from her face as she contemplated. She did not answer him, but he sat down next to her anyway. They both looked up at The Sky for a moment before he gathered the courage to speak up again. Ross mentioned how he missed it up there and that he was happy to be going home in a few days. Then he asked why she was not speaking to him. Arden sat up. "You know why."

"I came here as soon as I could to apologize. Come on, you know me, Arden. You've known me since we were children." He started to smile as he reminisced. "Remember when I sat near you in Energy class? I had the biggest crush on you. One time, I wrote you a love letter but I kept it in my library book. I cursed myself when I accidentally turned it back into the library where the next person would see it." He turned a little red. He was wearing his warrior vest, his Striker tassel was tied proudly to his well-defined bicep.

He looks good…really good, Arden begrudgingly thought to herself. When his coloring went back to a normal tan, she could not tell he was wounded, except the limp. It would eventually go away in time—at least, that's what Dr. Koy told him. "Was the library book called *Sky Law Terms*?" He frowned. "I was that next person. I got the letter but before I could say anything, you transferred to the warrior classes. I wanted to see you but you were doing boot camp."

He shook his head in embarrassment and then laughed. "I didn't realize you knew. You are the one I planned to court. I asked my father when I was fifteen for his blessing before I pursued you and tried to win over your uncle.

When I was assigned to be your warrior, I was relieved that *finally* everything was falling into place. Then I fell at the Flying Festival and you…fell for a human." That comment lingered in the air for several moments. Ross adjusted his warrior vest and then continued, "What luck is that? I tried to tell you last evening, before you kicked me out of your room, that I could hear you two play out every single night while I was stuck in bed, a bed that felt like a prison. I wanted to be the one to spend time with you, to drink with you at night and take you for walks. I tried to play it off and pretended I knew nothing. Pretend I didn't hear you in his bed talking late at night, the kissing, or the heavy breathing…." He took a deep breath. "Anyway, I just had to let you know that I never meant to hurt you. I was delirious from the fever."

She shrugged her shoulders. "I apologize that you had to hear that. I don't know if it is love that I feel for Myth, but it is *something* sacred. I will admit that you are the Sky Walker that I hoped I would end up with. I just don't know, Ross. I am *not* extremely happy with you right now. I know you didn't mean to hurt me, but I am scarred *forever* because of your violence." She cleaned the dirt off her hands. "Best thing about you right now is your dog." They both snickered. "Where is Solar, by the way?" she asked.

"Solar made a friend, they are playing back at the camp. I am so glad I found him on my way here. I'm told he is a mutt but predominantly Australian Shepherd."

"Whatever that means." She giggled.

Suddenly, his face became serious as he turned to examine Arden. He touched her face then reached for her scarred arm. "May I see the damage?"

She thought about it quickly and then surrendered her deformed limb. He started at her hand to see the deep shiny scars and protruding veins. His eyes became glistened as he moved on to her wrist. She shivered in pain to his touch. Carefully lifting up her sleeve, he examined the rest of her arm, moved up to her shoulder, and, finally, her neck. He placed his forehead on top of her head. She could feel her hair getting damp as he let go of unshed tears, overwhelmed with guilt. She started to soften and muttered for him to please stop crying. He wiped away his tears. Reluctantly, she grabbed his hand and placed a small kiss on it. They sat in silence. All those sweet and thoughtful words of childhood and their possible future flew through her mind. Those tears were for her. She then grabbed his face with her scarred hand and looked him dead in the eye. A small but long kiss was placed on his reddened cheek. She slowly inched closer toward him as he closed his eyes. Arden's lips met his. They kissed softly as she got lost in this confusion of wanting him but wanting to keep him at a distance. He pulled her closer and laid her on her back in one swift motion. He did not care that they were out in the open or if anyone would see their display of love. After moments passed, he simply gazed at her heart-shaped face. She finally whispered the word *forgiven*.

*****

Arden decided that she needed the rest of the evening to be alone and to self-reflect. Although she cared for Ross, she was not "all in." Her heart was still back at The Hard Road in the hands of a stubborn human. In time she would take it back, but she did not have the strength to do it yet. Reaching her bedroom, she noticed an envelope was tucked under her door. She opened the lovely scented envelope and pulled out a handwritten letter.

> Arden,
>
> I am on the mend. No worries. I will explain when you get back home. Be careful and trust only Dekker. Thank you for helping me. I am forever in your debt.
>
> Love,
> Ellery

This brought a smile on her face and a tear to her eye. She sat down on her bed and opened her bag. She placed the letter in it for safekeeping. She felt her hand brush against Myth's badge, making her cringe. The stolen badge laid in her hand as she read out loud, "Runner." It was exquisite. The colors, material, and sewing were of the finest quality. Further examining it, she noticed a small script toward the bottom of the threaded material. Squinting her almond eyes, she finally made out the words. "Marco Rockwell." She punched her scarred fist into her mattress and cursed loudly. "Really? Of all the badges I could have stolen, I stole his dead brother's? Great job, Arden. Brilliant."

Her feet hit the ground and she started pacing on her wool rug with bare feet dirty from a day in the dirt. Her head shook back and forth as she tried to figure out a way to take it back to him. She decided that she would write him a letter of apology enclosed with the badge and have a mail person take it to him. Resting down on her bed, she pulled out *Vintage Lovely*. She eyed it for a moment and felt almost as if it was mocking her. As if it was sticking out its tongue and antagonizing her. Perhaps ripping the book apart page by page and watching it burn would be satisfying to her soul? *Ugh! Boys make things super hard.* Myth and Ross managed to turn her world upside down in record time. She did not even know that was possible, yet here she was with a broken heart by Myth and Ross was trying to glue it back together. Ross was the breath of normalcy in a world that was not normal. Ross was real and seemed everlasting. Her hand opened the book to the view of the inscription that she was now familiar with. "M. E. Cottonwood," it read. Reading a few pages of this book made her drowsy. She was asleep before she knew it.

*****

Fog covered the dark evening grounds as unknown insects made noises into the night. Arden's feet marched through the weeds on a mission. She spotted her friend walking up a hill with jovial energy. "This time around, I'm not letting Arkin get away with this," she told herself. A large tree was in the distance and a shadow of a person was under it. She sprinted as fast as she could to reach her. Ellery's laughter echoed throughout the woods and into Arden's head. Arden felt like she was going to faint. She fell down on one knee. "No, I will stop him!" she announced. Her eyes were glued to the happy couple who were kissing in the moonlight. She was waiting for it to go wrong, waiting for him to make his move. On the prowl, she crept in closer, ignoring the dizziness in her head. The breeze picked up and she noticed that Ellery got cold. Arkin pulled her closer to him to warm her up. They started down a path in the woods. She followed close behind until they reached a wooden cabin. Arkin told Ellery to get inside and get comfortable. Arden ran up to the side of the cabin. A blurry window showed Ellery's silhouette lying on a makeshift bed on the floor. Candlelight shined in the dark. Arden looked around for a weapon and quickly found a tree branch. She slowly stepped around the corner of the cabin to watch the perpetrator. Arkin was nowhere to be found as a heavy fog surrounded Arden. Suddenly, she heard a scream inside the cabin that reverberated into her soul.

*****

"Class, what would you call this, again?" Professor Greiner asked the students in her room. Clad in a red plaid dress with black stockings and boots, she wore her long blonde hair in a high bun. She was a mystery teacher who spoke of puzzles in great wonder and enthusiasm. The class was a combination of history, mystery, and investigating.

Arden's hand rose eagerly. Greiner pointed at her. "It's a globe of the world." Arden was looking at all the countries shaded in different colors. She was baffled by the places she had never heard of and oceans she had never seen. People speaking different languages completely foreign to her was like a fairy story in a cloud book.

"Yes, it's a globe. Sadly, not all these countries are inhabited anymore due to wars and Mother Nature. Let's just say, humankind had been wiped out in many places. Moreover, many areas have been condemned under Adao's Sky Laws. We call these areas wastelands. Humans are a dying breed these days and now vanishing daily. We must stay strong." Ms. Greiner sat back down at her desk with an impassive look on her face. Fixing the glasses on her face, she sighed then waved for people to leave the classroom. She stayed in a silent daze as people made their way out the classroom. Students were shrugging their shoulders and whispering on their way out.

"What's wrong with her?" a young male Sky Walker asked inquisitively.

"It's like she doesn't understand Adao's reasons or something," said another.

"I think she's crazy," whispered another.

Arden stayed seated. She was not going anywhere, she wanted to pick the mind of this professor. Arden stood up slowly after everyone walked out of the classroom and made her way to her desk timidly. Playing with her claws, she asked shyly, "Miss Greiner, are you okay?" Arden was worried for the silent teacher.

Miss Greiner lifted her head and gave smile to Arden, a fake one that showed off her beautiful red lipstick and perfect teeth. "I think so."

Grabbing her steaming hot coffee-cola, she took a sip and placed it down on her wooden coaster. She did not seem to mind the drops that had fallen onto her dress. "I have seen many things in this world. I have heard many stories. I have investigated many cases. Sometimes, even I become surprised by the turn of events." She sat back in a relaxed way and shook her head from side to side.

"Would you help me understand?"

This made Greiner laugh aloud but in a soft manner. "You wouldn't understand."

Arden sat down next to her professor and said, "Try me?"

Greiner smirked at her and muttered, "Do I dare? Convince me on why I should reveal my thoughts to you."

Arden dug deep and unleashed her true feelings. "King Oswin was my father. King Adao is my uncle. I am the daughter and niece of royalty in The Sky but I do not relish it. In fact, I believe my uncle is doing more harm than good. I do not know the extent of it, but I know enough. I see darkness in my uncle's words and actions when others see light. I must know whether my feelings really hold water or not. Can you assist me?"

Professor Greiner's eyes widened in fascination and wonder. Under her breath, she said, "Arden…are you Arden?" Arden nodded confidently. "Well then…yes, I've been waiting for you. Follow me."

Greiner walked out of the room and down the long hallway. They passed by Sky Walkers and humans walking the halls. She followed the professor down corridors until they reached an enormous, echoing library with scarlet walls, the L. Ward's Library. A banner read, "Write for life." There was no one to be found here in this grand, glorious place. Greiner turned and sat down in an overstuffed chair near a roaring fireplace. The blue-gray fireplace was made of slate and was almost as big as the entire wall. Arden got situated in a twin seat nearby.

"First of all, what questions do you have for me?" She sat there almost like an open book herself.

"I'll start with language. I wonder why my kind speaks the same language as some humans. How would that even happen if Sky Walkers had lived in The Sky this whole time?"

Professor Greiner thought for a moment before responding. "Have you heard of a myth?" Just the word *myth* made Arden's hair stand on end. She shook her head, swaying her brilliant blue feathers. Greiner explained that a myth was a traditional tale, a story in early history that typically involved extraordinary beings doing extraordinary things. "There is a myth about your people, the Sky Walkers—amazing beings who are part human and part phoenix—have lived here on Earth many, many years ago. I believe that something terrible happened, making them flee for The Sky and build a world away from the 'barbaric' humans."

Arden's eyebrows rose as she said, "That would explain the language being the same as most humans, English.

How would they flee though? It is not as if Sky Walkers can actually fly or they would not use their phoenix?"

The professor smiled brightly. "Just because *you* can't fly doesn't mean that it wasn't possible at one time. Arden, I believe you are innocently blinded." She stoked the bright and beautiful fire before she continued. "There are very few Sky Walkers who currently live here on Earth."

Arden jumped back and stared at her in disbelief. "It is not possible that Sky Walkers live on Earth or Adao would have them killed. Their family would have noticed that they were missing. Sky Walkers just do not disappear. Humans disappear."

Greiner eyed Arden. "Well, you can disagree all you want, but I have actually seen a Sky Walker live as a human. I have only seen one but I have heard of at least one other. Think of it this way, if they lived here once upon a time, perhaps not *all* the Sky Walkers followed the queen. Anything is possible."

This perked Arden up. She thought, *If there is another Sky Walker living on Earth, then why couldn't she?*

"Arden, don't go getting any ideas and hope to stay. Even though a few have been known to live off our land, it's quite another thing for royalty to relocate."

Arden played it off and laughed aloud in agreement. "Why would humans be so upset by my father coming down if they have seen a Sky Walker before?"

Ms. Greiner wagged a finger in her face. "Just because a Sky Walker lives down here doesn't mean they don't try hard to blend in. Just so happen, I was able to see a Sky Walker through a window when their guard was down.

I believe they live in the woods and are in hiding." This conversation opened Arden's mind. She did not realize there was even the possibility of her kind living amongst the humans. The question would be why. Why would they leave The Sky? "I'm sure you have heard of Queen Araline, right?"

"Yes, I used to dress up as Queen Araline when I was young. She was the heroine in my favorite cloud book."

"I firmly believe Queen Araline existed though very different from your fairytale. I've researched her a lot in my lifetime. I believe she was a goddess of good but also evil. She ruled her people down here on Earth before moving everyone to The Sky. The goddess said, 'I cannot witness my people being judged by humankind any longer. I will sacrifice my wings for a new land of promise.' Then they flew to The Sky and built a world. In another version, some researchers say that the goddess purposely cracked sections of the Earth and forced gravity to raise the land way up above. She sang a curse song to the humans below and then lived on the land that floated above. Queen Araline said, 'I shall deliver my people to a land where we shall not perish.'"

Arden took some time to think through the myths about her people. A few moments later, she noticed that the professor was nodding off to sleep right there in front of the warm fire. She stood up and viewed the beautiful library once more. She wanted to take in the beauty since she will be heading home in just a few days. Arden walked past the professor when a hand grabbed hers. Greiner's eyes were still closed but she spoke aloud as if awake. "Keep him at arm's length, Arden. You know nothing of his evil." Her hand let go and dropped to her side.

An uneasy feeling radiated down Arden's body, startled by the ominous message. She strolled out the library and shut the door firmly behind her. Arden walked up to the front desk with an envelope in her hand. She said a small prayer to God that the badge would get to Myth safely. Sealing the envelope, she looked around for a friendly face.

Bianca looked up from a book in her hand and grinned. She gracefully moved around the counter, gave Arden a small hug, and greeted her with a bright hello. "What do you need? I would love to assist you." Arden handed the envelope to Bianca and told that it was extremely important that it get to The Hard Road immediately. Bianca made an uncertain face. "I will send it out with our footman but I can't promise the speed." She walked her way back behind the counter when Arden noticed the book she had in her hand with a very familiar cover of lace and roses. *Vintage Lovely.*

"Bianca, I have that same book! Do you like it?"

Redness developed on her sweet cheeks and she nodded. "It's amazing and beautiful and…well, you know." They both giggled aloud.

"By the way, my book has a person's name in it, M. E. Cottonwood. Do you know any Cottonwoods down here?"

Her innocent face lit up and she spoke softly, "Yes, of course. That name is very well-known down here."

Arden was intrigued. "Do you know anyone with the initials ME?"

Again, Bianca spoke softly as if she was telling a secret. "Yes, Mary Ella Cottonwood was a famous writer for a secret newspaper here in Chillicothe, Ohio. This was years ago when I was a child. Mary Ella got into some trouble and was banished into a nearby wasteland."

"Why would Sky Walkers banish her?"

The girl shook her head. "Not Sky Walkers. It was the humans who banished her."

Wow! Arden did not realize that the humans banished people too. "I wonder which wasteland?"

Bianca had the answer to that. "It's up north from here, where Columbus used to be. Now it is just soil and turned down buildings. I am not even sure if she survived it. I feel bad for her though. It is tough enough to have the Sky King on her back, let alone, the humans against her too."

"Wait a minute! Bianca, why would she have Adao on her back?"

The young woman's face had fallen some. "She was banished because of her love affair."

Arden quickly asked, "With whom?" even though she knew the answer.

"King Adao."

Chapter 15

KNOCK, KNOCK! ARDEN lifted her head up as her knotted hair stood up in clumps. Her eyes squinted to see what time it was. Her domed bracelet read six o'clock. She stretched her arms and grunted. Her feet found the floor and she walked to the door sluggishly. "Who is it?" she croaked.

"Tess. Let me in."

A smirk spread on Arden's face as she quickly opened the door. Tess walked in carrying a garment bag in one hand and a cardboard box in another. Arden shut the door and faced Tess with an amused look on her face. "What is all this and why so darn early?" She rubbed her sleepy eyes.

Tess threw the garment bag onto the bed. "So I have a special dress for you to wear tomorrow night. Typically, I have assorted dresses for everyone to pick through, but I want to give you a special one to wear. I hope you're okay with that." Tess beamed, her eyes bright.

"*Gee!* I don't know if I am going, honestly. There is too much in my head right now. I appreciate you thinking of me though."

Tess put her hand resolutely on her waist. "You are going, that is the end of it. It is a perfect ending to your bizarre journey. Am I right or am I right?" She had to admit that Tess seemed wise beyond her years. "I have a feeling you will like it. It reminds me of you. Just look at it once I'm gone. I left a little note inside the bag too. See ya!" Tess made her way out the door and slammed it behind her. *Sometimes that girl is full of grace and other times she absolutely is not. She stood looking at the unopened dress.*

Decisively, Arden started to unzip the bag with ease pulling out the sacred material in its entirety. Her scarred hand closed over her mouth in awe. It was breathtaking! It's like nothing she had ever seen before. As brilliant white lace cascaded down to the floor. Parts of the dress was semi-transparent but most of it was made from the softest of lace. "This is a masterpiece and must be vintage," she began talking to herself.

Arden held the dress against her body and viewed herself in the full-length mirror. She had to try it on! She practically jumped out of her night robe and slid the dress over her head. It cascaded down her body and the fit her magnificently, hanging on her hips just the right way. *Perfect!* The dress swirled around her as she viewed her back in the mirror and attempted to zip the dress up. The sleeves were long and tapered off at the back of her hands. Arden's lightly tanned skin peeped through in places but was still classy. The back of the dress was very low cut, barely covering up her bottom. For a second, she was speechless. Then she tightened a thin white belt against her flat stomach. She discovered two Velcro-like tape hidden on her chest. When they were pulled, a section of the dress came off, transforming a humble classic to super sexy dress in seconds. Her cleavage were definitely on display without it. She looked down thoughtfully. She would have to decide which look she would want to take to this dance, conservatively demure or a sassy vintage. Either way, it was vintage lovely. Arden made eye contact with herself in the mirror. *Vintage lovely.*

She still couldn't believe King Adao. A darkness crept over her. *Who does he think he is? He condemns and kills humans but falls in love with one?* "Hypocrite!" she yelled to no one.

Taking the dress off, she laid it down on the bed. Her thoughts were flooding her mind and she remembered asking Bianca to try to get more information about his love affair. Why else would he have a human sex book with a woman's name in it. She realized a major plus to this. If he loved a human, then how could he judge her for loving one also? If he judged her, then so be it. She was tired of making sure he approved everything and sick to death of walking on egg shells. Tucking the dress safely back into the bag, she looked for the note Tess left her. She held it up and started to read the words aloud.

> Arden,
>
> This dress has been in my family for many, many generations. My mother told me to keep it even though I will never be married. Yes, it is a wedding dress. The women who molded me into what I am today had all worn this dress. It felt

> most appropriate to have you wear it. You remind me of them.
>
> You saved my little sister. I will never be able to repay you for that. Please take this dress as a gift. I wanted to write this since I suck at talking about my feelings and whatnot.
>
> —Tess, aka Spitter

Arden sat down on her bed naked and vulnerable. She reread the letter a few times. Wiping away a tear in the corner of her eye, she placed the letter in her personal bag for safekeeping, right on top of the Hanging by a Thread T-shirt. She had almost forgotten about the cardboard box Tess left on her nightstand. It contained blush-colored, high-heeled shoes. Arden's eyes grew in curiosity. *How does one walk in these?* She held one in her hand, felt the weight of it, and noticed there were diamonds along the heel and toe. It was glorious and looked like a piece of art. Her face was red with excitement, she could not wait to tell someone. She went looking for Ross. Maybe he would be her date for this occasion.

She walked down the hallway to the door that read "Mud Pie" and tapped lightly. The door swung open. Ross stood tall in the doorway, wearing no shirt and a vague expression. Looking past him, she noticed that he was using his domed band to project Sky News on his wall. He motioned for her come in. She made herself comfortable on his bed next to a sleeping puppy named Solar. Solar's beautiful fur was a mixture of gray, white, black, and tan and his eyes were a brilliant blue. He made small whimpering sounds as he slept. "What's going on in The Sky?" she asked, attempting to break the ice.

He sat down near her and said, "Not much. You know, same boring stuff. Ravel Reed is coming out with a new book. That was the big news of the day." His eyes analyzed her.

"Remember our first night at The Hard Road? I told you that you reminded me of Ravel Reed. That was a compliment."

He turned the news off. "I do remember that. I guess it is a compliment. But you do realize that he just writes cloud books, right?"

Arden looked amused by his foul mood and said, "So?"

Agitation radiated off him as he continued, "I mean, he's writing make-believe stories. While real men are fulfilling their protective duty, your Mr. Reed is safely inside his house writing the woes of a middle-aged Sky Walker. It's just a little pathetic."

Arden gasped and had the urge to smack the stubble right off his confident face. "For one, you sound just like Adao, which is not a compliment. Two, I respect and love our warriors. You shouldn't belittle others to make yourself feel better. And three, writers have an amazing ability that you do not. They can take me to worlds that I wish existed and fill my wildest dreams. Never underestimate the power of the mind and the written word."

He moved over to a desk chair to look Arden in the face. "*Wow!* You are defending writers over warriors? The niece of royalty, everyone. Adao must be super proud."

Jealousy was written all over his face. "By the way, who says I can't fulfill your wildest desires? Think about it. I know I do every damn night." She shook her head, she will not participate in these weird love games. As if he sensed it, he changed the subject. "About that first night, was that the first time you've seen Myth?" She nodded. "So he ended up not wanting you, right?"

Sensing another attempt to argue, Arden stood up quickly and hissed, "What is with you?" She spoke through gritted teeth.

"Well, you've been ignoring me lately. I must say, I don't appreciate it. You need to make some damn decisions, Arden. Be decisive. Either you want me or you do not. I do not do 'in between'."

An exasperated sigh burst out of her as she looked at the ceiling. *Great, here comes another lecture from a male!* There was one boy who could not take "the hard road" with her, now this one who cannot do "in between". She decided that she clearly did not need either of them. She walked over to him. "One day it's my *childhood crush* speaking sweetly to me, next day it's *psycho Ross* coming to attack and burn me, and now its *melodramatic, jealous Ross*. That is way too many Ross in this equation. I'm done." His eyes became dark. She dared him to say one more thing or even touch her so she would bite his head off.

"Well, that's me. I gave you my heart and you put it in your back pocket. I am sick of being put off then led on. If you do not really like me, then I am moving on. Hell, I will leave tonight if you want me to. I wasted too many years on you." He threw a shirt on over his head and muttered, "I've been aching to get back to work anyways."

Arden could not resist and blurted out, "Yeah! Oh, and let's not forget *Striker Ross*. That's another twisted side of you too." He stumbled back and glared at her. "I know what that tassel around your arm truly represents. You couldn't have been a Scout and just work the grounds. You could have chosen to be a Scoper and stay at The Sky. You had to pick Striker, didn't you? Fitting, it seems."

His jaw clenched and did not speak for a moment. Fletcher was right all along. "I demand to know who told you!"

"No!" Arden stood her ground.

"That is classified information. And for your information, I was chosen for it. I didn't pick it."

Arden looked him up and down and walked out the door. It was a silent goodbye.

*****

This poetry writing class was really starting to get to her. She did enjoy the lecture on Lord Tennyson and had written a poem based off his work. "I have a poem for you all. As we discussed Camelot, I wanted to read a poem that one of your fellow Sky Walkers wrote. It captures the struggle of Lady Shallot's curse." Suddenly Arden's words filled the small squared room.

The Lady of Shalott
by Arden Ivy Kress

Lullaby echoes through the darkness from above.
Her voice, like no other, she sings of only love.
Lust and infatuation she does not know but yearns for,
While watching in her mirror and her singing to soar!

A castle so harsh and cold, she needs to be free
To make love to a man and for Lady Shalott to be!
To escape her horrid curse that seals her in dull towers,
She wants to believe that she can dance with the flowers,
To run wildly in the meadows with another beautiful soul.
To do all that is superb will bring a God-awful toll!

Suddenly, he appears galloping on a strong black horse.
Her bright eyes glare out the window with such great force.
Oh my! The mirror shatters, the curse is becoming worse.
As he comes closer and closer, her heart begins to burst!
Her flowing dress thrashing down the hall with haste.
The sudden feeling of burden and now have to chase?

She needs this male in her life, why so badly?
So she flew out the castle to a shallow stream, sadly.
Thinking she will not meet him, "It's too late, I know."
She spots an abandoned boat and sets out to row.
Singing lightly her death song with fury and love,
Is this better than being in that tower up above?

To sing my last song for a man I know not.
Why did this creature come to me and my feelings not fought?
She was adrift, slowly steering toward Camelot.

Suddenly, her vision began to grow blurry like a white snowy night.
Out of breath, she became and then her view in bright light.
To die, but for this life she will not fight.
For she lived not a life, though she lived for that knight.

The class clapped their hands and some even stood up for her. She turned around to see everyone truly tuned in to everything she said. Nodding discreetly was her way of showing appreciation. It was liberating and embarrassing.

"Before we end class, you have one last homework. Write a poem about something you have experienced down here on Earth. Remember, honesty is a beautiful thing. Place it in my work tray tomorrow morning by ten."

She grabbed her books, walked out the classroom door with a sense of purpose and newfound pride. As rain drizzled from The Sky, Arden sat on a bench and let Mother Nature pour down on her, fully soaking her. The atmosphere felt thick and The Sky was a dark gray color. Night was approaching, she welcomed it. This rain made her feel free and she needed it. Nature's pure medicine for the soul and mind. The rain started to pour harder and harder. Lightning and thunder screamed across The Sky She was suddenly inspired to write a poem in her mind.

Freedom is Not Overrated
by Arden Kress

I know its freedom, I can taste it.
Adventure, I smell it.
I'm on my own and I know it.

It is the beginning of a long journey,
and I am ready for it.
Earth is a canvas,
And I am about to leave a huge
emotional impression on it.
It will be my art, I am sure of it.

Trying to grow and be myself,
Trying to hold on to my innocence as well.
I will not free it.
It is bottled up inside me and I am carrying it.
Carrying it in my travels around
this crazy, hurdled Earth.
And I will jump it.

Clouds are rolling, thunder screaming,
Lightening stretches itself across the breeze,
I can feel it.
Feeling free is the state of mind for me.
I will live it.

She thought it was ironic that she felt freer on Earth where freedom was forcefully taken from the people. She could not lie to herself, she admired humans. She found them interesting, impactful, and knowledgeable. Each place felt like home but also strangely not. Arden was starting to be honest with herself more and more. She loved and hated the fact that this fantastic adventure would come to an end soon. *Was it wrong to dread going back to the normal, boring life of a Sky Walker?* Earth made her feel alive. It gave her a new appreciation for the world, a real world. Home now felt like a glorious world of facades and lies. The very man who guided and ruled over his people was oppressing the humans, a dictator. These feelings rushed to the surface, causing her to feel guilt. She flet privileged and guilty for it.

The door closed behind her, echoing throughout L. Ward's Library. She swept the room to see a few Sky Walkers in the back of the library and Professor Greiner sitting next to the fireplace. She walked toward her and greeted her with a hello.

Greiner stood up and grabbed Arden's hand. "Good to see you. You ready for tomorrow?" She spoke softly.

"I suppose. May I join you for a few minutes? I have a few questions for you so I'm going to be blunt. The last time I saw you, you told me to keep 'him' at arm's length and spoke of 'his' evil. Who were you referring to?" Arden sat back fully into her seat, trying to get comfortable.

A concerned look quickly showed on the professor's face. "My dear, why ask a question you know the answer to? I will not answer what you already know."

Arden nodded her head and said, "Adao."

The professor crossed her legs and looked deep into Arden's eyes. "I see bright things in your future. I see many things. But you...you are different."

"Thank you." Fumbling through her mind, she finally asked the biggest question. "Would you be willing to help me investigate something?" Greiner did not answer but motioned for her to continue. "I want to know exactly what happened to Mary Ella Cottonwood. Do you know the name?"

"Indeed, I do. She was an undercover writer for this area. Mary Ella caught the attention of King Adao. He visited her quite often and threatened her to stop with her writing. All I know is that she went too far with her daring articles and their love-hate affair. It is said they had a real relationship though. Last I heard, she was living in a wasteland called Tamarisk, formerly known as Columbus. I know nothing else on the matter." *Tamarisk?* Arden thought. "Tamarisk is a type of tree whose leaves our ancestors used for healing. Since it does not bear fruit, it is associated with bad luck. They say those who go to Tamarisk have bad luck."

It made sense to her now. Arden convinced Professor Greiner to help her investigate more details and instructed her to report to Fletcher at The Landing. After giving her a hug and thanking her, Arden left the library and decided to get some sleep. After all, the big dance was tomorrow!

Chapter 16

IT WAS A sunny, bright spring day and many people were outside enjoying the weather. Since this was the last day of camp, no one had official classes. It was a day to pack your belongings, get a certificate for participating, and then dance the night away. They were all making memories that would last forever. Arden was happy she got to experience it.

Earlier when Arden woke up, she laid out everything she would wear for the dance tonight: dress, shoes, jewelry, makeup, lotion, and hair clips. She decided to be conservative and wear the dress with the additional material. She was nervous about dancing but at least she learned some human dance moves. Tess and Dekker would be there so she felt better about it. Dekker already visited her this morning and talked about the clothing he had to wear called a tuxedo. He wanted to see her dress but she would not let him because she wanted it to be a surprise. He settled for a nice breakfast with his good friend. He talked about all the classes he took, his favorite class was Mysteries. He thought Professor Greiner was "super hot" for a human, apparently picking up the human slang. This made them laugh and bond over fruit and seeds. Conversation was easy with Dekker. Everything felt doable and normal with him in her life. He was a constant support that she was thankful for.

The day went fast. She had finished reading a human book when she realized the time. She had one hour to get ready and get to the dance! She threw the time-sucking book across the room, jumped up, and showered in record time. Next, she lathered up in lotion and blow-dried her hair. The light danced off her shoes and wall as she sat on a desk to apply her makeup. Since she was playing it safe with her dress, she decided to wear some dramatic makeup. Her smoky eyes were made with charcoal black and dabs of shimmer. The rose-colored blush made her cheekbones prominent and a nude lipstick pulled the look together. Her eyelashes fanned out in the most perfect way that brought her some confidence. It was now 6:45 p.m. and she was supposed to be at the dance in fifteen minutes. She took a deep breath and looked in the mirror at the nearly unrecognizable face staring back at her. It felt good to dress up and feel more like a human. Her hair was brushed and curled, and she placed a ruby barrette on her left side. Her hair was extremely long these days, only an inch from her bottom. Her beautiful blue feathers were as vibrant as ever and complimented the dress. The lacy dress slid down her body like velvet. She felt fortunate and honored to wear such a historical and sentimental piece. Pulling her high-heeled shoes on her feet was the last step to getting ready for this night. She practiced walking in her room for a few minutes. She spritzed some perfume on both sides of her neck. Stepping back and looking at herself all done up was nerve-racking. She was impressed and hoped others would like it too. She turned her desk lamp on and grabbed a small purse that held her lipstick and domed bracelet. She walked out the door and into the dark night.

The sound of her high-heeled shoes echoed throughout the long hallways. She was becoming a professional in these things. She passed people huddled in groups that were talking about the camp and how they could not believe it was their last night. At times, hints of emotions could be heard in their voices. Arden realized right then that this camp experience meant a lot to others too, not just her. All the Sky Walkers learned of a world they were raised to dislike. She wondered if they had seen the disconnect too. Before they knew it, they would be back at The Sky filled with a hierarchy for the rest of their lives. Her gown slightly dragged on the floor as she made her way toward the gymnasium. The stillness of the night was now upon her. She had a full evening ahead of her. She heard soft music in the distance. It echoed throughout her body. She closed her eyes tightly in a dreamlike state and thought of the swaying of people, glasses clinking, lustful glances, simple chatter, chilled drinks, satin dresses, floral aromas, and overall beauty filling the room. As she neared the gymnasium doors, she had to blink her eyes repeatedly for them to adjust to such a glorious setup.

The party looked like something from The Sky…but better. The theme was "A Night's Dream." All the lights were off save for strands of twinkling lights that were hung at the tent ceiling and some candles of all sizes placed strategically to produce soft, dramatic lighting. Lovely shooting stars dangled from the dark overhead ceiling. A grand silver stage was to the left of the room decorated with flowers. She had never seen so many flowers in one room in her life. In the middle of the room was a huge fountain a fast-flowing waterfalls the clear water that glowed in the light. Its focal point was a statue of a Sky Walker who reminded her of Queen Araline. *How can this camp afford such lavish things?* She moved further inside and walked around the gigantic room to take it all in. Willow trees were brought in with strands of lights dangling on the branches to add a whimsical feel. Arden truly felt like she was in a dream as everything swirled around her. The smell of cigars and moss filled the air as she finally made it back to the entrance. Taking a deep breath, she fixed her hair with her talons and reapplied some lip gloss in a corner.

"Excuse me, attention everybody! Please join us around the stage as we get this evening started," Tess' voice echoed over a microphone. Chatter started to decease as humans and Sky Walkers merged together toward the stage. She had not realized there were so many people at this camp. Tess smiled to the crowd. She wore a daring black sleeveless top that had a built-in neck choker, a camel-colored skirt cut just above her knee, and long black boots up her legs. She continued, "We are so happy to have you all here tonight to celebrate a memorable night. What is funny is that not only do the Sky Walkers take something back with them, but we humans here at camp take something too. It is an experience for us all and we, the humans, have are happy this camp exists. It has been an honor because we learn a lot from you as well. We may be enemies most days, but I have hope that you will not forget this time of peace. Now it is time to hear from *your* king, King Adao."

Arden knew that Tess did not care for Sky Walkers all that much, but she knew how to work a crowd. A roar of cheers reverberated throughout the venue. Sky Walkers clapped with devotion as everyone watched a huge screen descend from the ceiling in a slow manner. It showed King Adao waving to his people.

He cleared his throat and began, "My dear people, I hope you have enjoyed this little educational vacation there on Earth. Your family and friends of The Sky have missed you. As our Sky Laws state, 'Gather together, my Sky Walkers, for we are one under God.' When you return, you will have two days off from your legal life. You are expected to get back to school after that and back to your sole purpose, The Sky Laws and justice. Speaking of justice, I wanted to provide an update on a fellow Sky Walker who was harmed during her stay there. She has since fully recovered. We are investigating what happened. I do not take this lightly. In closing, please enjoy your last evening on Earth. I will see you all soon."

In unison, everyone held out their hands and pointed their chins to the ceiling in prayer. King Adao's handsome face disappeared. Arden had to admit that she somehow missed him. A lot. Weak guilt surfaced a little but she quickly put that to rest as she noticed Tess coming up on stage again.

"*Ahem!* Before we get this party started, I want to thank King Adao for sending such amazing flowers, food, and decorations for this event. The first song of the night is for your traditional dance. MUSIC!" she barked and everyone stood still when the first song played. A series of bird chirps and harps filled the room. Suddenly, the people of The Sky repositioned to the center of the dance floor and prepared to show the humans their traditional dance to jump-start the night.

Arden took her assigned place in front of everyone since she was royalty. She clapped her hands sharply as a signal for everyone to start moving. The music had a Celtic feel to it. The famous song was called "The Bold and Brave." Her arms reached out, gracefully swayed up and down, and made a small step to the right and left. Then she snapped her fingers. Every move was executed with purpose and grace similar to a ballerina. Some moves were swanlike in elegance. There were no sudden movements, just swaying limbs that complimented the music. It was peaceful and majestic. Everyone clapped in unison when the song was done. People came up to Arden and gave her hugs. She smiled, starting to feel a little more comfortable. She searched the crowd for Dekker, scanning face after face. Finally, she spotted him near the food table. She should had known. The table had silver platters on them and was stacked with the best of foods. Large vases of flowers and greenery were the centerpiece. Dekker had a handful of food, bobbing his head to an upbeat human song. He was dressed in a black tuxedo and looked very charming. She made her way to him as they made eye contact. His face froze and his lips formed an *O*. When she reached him, she placed a small kiss on his cheek.

"There you are! Good evening, sir." She smiled brightly and gave a bow in a joking way.

Dekker laughed. "You are the most gorgeous thing I've ever seen." He hugged her tightly and shook his head in disbelief while eyeing her up and down. "I'm speechless... seriously!" Her face started to turn as red as rubies. Being classy, she tried to cover up her blush. Dekker made her twirl, so he could see the back. Her blue feathers was a blur in the wind as she twirled. "Too bad Mythias isn't here to see you, *aye*?" That name sent a shiver down her back.

"I'm glad he's not here, I do not need him. I don't need anybody." Her voice was instantly cold.

This surprised Dekker. He shrugged his shoulders and muttered an "okay" then a "sorry" for bringing his name up. She grinned softly at him, grabbed his hand, and pulled him to the dance floor. They circled each other and chuckled as they tried to dance in a human way. She grabbed the side of her dress and pulled it up. This helped her dip down and really be free. Out of nowhere, hands came from behind her and covered her eyes. Arden swung around quickly to see Bianca's elated face. "I'll dance with you too!"

The three friends used kinetic dancing moves. Kinetics was a modern form of dance that Arden practiced, thanks to Tess. Speaking of Tess, she finally came from the crowd and joined the group. They bounced up and down in rhythm. Tess and Bianca would sing along to the songs. Dekker and Arden did not know the words to all these human songs.

After thirty minutes of dancing, drinking ginger spritzers, and eating some seeds, the first slow song of the night came on. Couples were making their way to the middle of the dance floor. It was a nice sight with the waterfalls near them. Surreal, even. Arden decided this was as good time as any to step outside to feel the cool air on her body. Her sweat instantly evaporated in such a chilly night. The bright, waxing gibbous moon hovered proudly in the dark sky and the stars shined as brightly as the ceiling inside. She took in the silence of the night.

After a while, she rejoined the party and found her group again. Dekker, Tess, and Bianca were back on the dance floor hitting it hard. The energy of the room was uplifting. This was probably the most fun she had ever experienced. Everyone looked gorgeous and seemed alive. Even the stiffest of Sky Walkers were letting loose and being wild. It was a great thing to watch. Abruptly, the music changed to a song that sounded very familiar to her. Her eyes widened when she realized it was the "Wild Things" song from The Hard Road. It immediately took her to another world too perfect to be played with the theme, A Night's Dream. She moved to the music and sang along with the lyrics. It was a powerful and meaningful song. The humans were fist pumping and singing loudly. It was an incredible thing. She swiftly realized that this was their anthem. It represented their people, and she loved it. Everything went in slow motion once the chorus rang loudly. She threw her hair back and moved her body along with the music. On the second verse, she quickly snapped out of it and felt eyes on her. She shifted her body from side to side, gazing out into the crowd around her. Just people dancing. She turned her body in a circle to get a better view.

There! Lurking in the shadow was a figure sitting a table dressed in dark clothing. Her heart stopped. *Could it be?* She squinted her eyes to focus in. It looked like it could be…Mythias? Ross? Hell, it may be Adao for all she knew. Courage stirred inside her and decided to march up to this stranger to see who it was. Her beautiful shoes marched to the back of the gym. When she finally made eye contact with this figure, a gasp escaped from her lips. "Mythias?"

"Yes," he replied.

She sat down next to him in disbelief. *I will not cry, I will not cry, I will not cry*, she thought repeatedly. Of course, it was Mythias. He was sitting the same exact way he did the first night she saw him at The Hard Road. He was slouched at a table looking mysterious in a dark corner. Same old Myth. "What are you doing here?" she barely got the words out before he stood up.

"Let's go. I need to talk to you." He stood tall above her in a quiet way.

She did not speak but walked out of the gym, down the hallway, and out the back door. Outside, she had her back to him. She could feel his presence behind her as she waited for him to speak. Folding her arms, she turned around to face the man who had broken her heart. "You here for your badge?"

"My badge?"

She looked down at her shoes. "I stole a badge of yours to remember you by. I accidentally took your brother's badge."

"I will need that back," he stated simply.

"I had a man deliver it to you. It should arrive any day now. I'm sorry. I promise you, I did not know it was his until it was too late. I didn't take it to hurt you or anything."

He shook his head in understanding, meaning it was okay. Mythias examined her face then his gaze swept down her body to her shoes. "You look beautiful," he muttered.

All she wanted to do was kiss him, hold him, and convince him to ask her to stay with him on Earth forever. It did not help that he was ravishingly handsome in a tuxedo. *Curses!* She wanted to blurt out all the information she found out about Adao and tell him there was a chance she could pull it off, but then it dawned on her that it would still be a "hard road" and that was not in the cards. So she stayed silent.

Mythias finally spoke. "You're probably wondering why I'm here. I'm not here for the badge, obviously." He stepped closer to her. "I'm here for you…" he trailed off shyly. All of a sudden, he grabbed her waist and kissed her passionately with just the right pressure.

Heat rose up to her face and she lost herself in the moment for only a few seconds. Then she pulled away. "Wait! Won't this make things harder?"

He kept his arms around her. "Arden, I thought that being with you would be too hard, but not being with you is an even harder road to travel. The hardest road I have ever known. I want to try this with you…if you will have me." She didn't say anything. Their eyes both revealed their souls and desire to be together. She glanced into the woods then grabbed his hand. She glided effortlessly into the nearby bushes and led him deeper into the night. Her dress was even brighter in the dark. He pulled her back to stop her. "I will lead."

They switched places as he now led, stepping over logs and avoiding thornbushes. They came upon a place that was nicely secluded. He removed his fancy black jacket slowly and laid it down on the mossy ground. It was spring, the promise of flowers were surrounding them. Arden gently pushed her hair back in a tie and dared to challenge him. She was not nervous at all. No, she was as calm as a winter's brook. She knew what she wanted and she was not going to hold back tonight. Not ever. Like revving engines, they were both eager to floor it but waiting for the right moment, the right signal. Arden made the first move. Remembering that this dress had a little trick to it, her hands found the Velcro ties and yanked them off like a bandage. This exposed much more of her skin. She was ready to take this step and show him all of her. She loved him. With every touch and every look, she knew he felt the same way. His hands found his way under her dress as he pulled her to him. She was all his. Just his touch made her swoon back and forth. Her right leg curled around his hip. She yearned to be closer to this beautiful being. He picked her up with ease and laid her down on his jacket. Her back laid flat, her dress spreading out to the sides. Crickets chirped in the distance and the lullaby of nature was their soundtrack. She had never felt this way before. He stroked her hair lovingly as they started to kiss passionately. As he leaned back, she began unbuttoning his crisp white shirt. She was proud that her chipped black talons were able to get around the buttons. When his pants were off, she realized it was her turn. But first, she admired and soaked him all up in an intimate way. This was the first moment she became nervous. Knowing she was going to bare herself to him out in the middle of nowhere was alluring. She rolled over onto her stomach for him to unzip her magnificent dress until only blue-laced panties covered her. His dark eyes looked hungry. He hung the dress and her panties on a branch high above them before promptly joining her. They clung to one another as if they would never let go. The night was all theirs so they took their time. They kissed, touched, and made love under the heavens. Only the moon joined them for this night—a night that fate arranged.

Hours later, they went back to camp and the dance was over. Their legs were shaky and weak as they walked through the halls. Trash was everywhere and no one was around. They really lost track of time, but it was very worth it. Myth had his arm around Arden as they walked to her room in a state of lust. They were dead tired so Arden just changed clothes and they jumped in bed to get some rest. Myth looked at Arden and whispered, "Thank you for the best night of my life." Then he closed his eyes.

Next morning, Arden opened her eyes weakly and stretched. A yawn immediately followed. Propping up on her elbow, she looked at Mythias who was half awake himself. She thought it had all been a dream. She realized that she was going home in about an hour. She wanted to wake up and go to bed next to him every single day of her life.

Mythias said, "I know you have to get ready to leave, but I want to say something. You make me feel alive and make me think that there is some good in the world. If the enemy in The Sky could produce an angel like you, then maybe there is hope after all. You are the gentle spark that I needed."

She sang softly while gathering up her belongings. She swept her hair up to the side then zipped up the now grass-stained, lace dress in the garment bag Tess provided. She threw on a pair of plain white underwear and a signature blue Sky Walker robe. Myth could not help but laugh at her when she kept Tess' combat boots and wore them secretly under her robe. Myth knew that Fletcher would be arriving any minute to take her home, but they had a plan. Arden was going to find a way back to The Hard Road in a few days, whether Fletcher helped her or not. It was easier for her to visit Earth than Myth going up to The Sky. Plus, Arden told him about King Adao's love affair, which have him just enough hope. A lot was on the line, but they would push forward. When they met again, they would come up with a long-term plan.

"I promise I'll be back. If needed, I will send messages through Fletcher. I do have to be careful. I will see you soon, Myth. I love you."

Myth smiled brightly for the first time in a long time. He pulled her close and whispered a sweet goodbye and an "I love you" in her ear.

When he left the room, she let out a large sigh. Placing her hands on her hips, she was deep in thought. She could not believe everything that happened. "Only on Earth," she said to herself and blushed the deepest color of crimson. She paused for a moment and realized that she had another poem inside her. She grabbed a sheet of paper and scribbled quickly, thinking of a future romantic night with Myth.

Call me Crimson
by Arden Kress

So call me Crimson. That is me.
The deepest color of red. The red that is me.
The shade of the rose he graced upon my face.
The color of the wine we drank from dawn to dusk.
The shade of our lips after being kissed
on when the romance struck.

So call me Crimson. That is me.
The color of the satin wrapped around
the curves of my womanly body.
The shade of the ruby ring that was placed on my finger.
The color on my nails that dared to linger.

So call me Crimson. That is me.
The deepest color of red. The red that is me.

She had everything packed, said farewell to her room as she exited, and walked down to the main area where Bianca worked. Sky Walkers were swarming everywhere, hugging the humans and thanking them for everything. Bianca cried when she hugged Arden. She also promised that she would work closely with Professor Greiner to find the truth behind "Adao and his wicked ways." Arden told

Bianca about Fletcher as the safest way to send a message to her in The Sky.

Tess stood in the background with her arms folded toughly. She waited patiently for Arden to be free. Arden made eye contact and they walked toward each other. "I see you survived Bianca's annoying ways?"

After Arden pulled away from their embrace, she said, "Give Bianca a break. She's going to do great things. She is a light in this darkness." Tess rolled her eyes. Arden continued, "Please tell Ivy about us being friends. I think she would have liked that. Also, I feel badly about taking this dress from you and…staining it." She held the garment bag high for Tess to inspect.

Tess shook her head. "Try to give that back to me and I will kill you."

Arden giggled. "Typical Tess. I will literally be looking over you and your world and praying for you. Maybe I will see you again…you never know."

Tess smiled with misty eyes and abruptly walked away.

Whew! This saying good-bye stuff was harder than Arden thought. Dekker told her that Fletcher was outside waiting for her so she waved to her friends and left. Fletcher was sitting patiently on Char. She took off running toward them. When she reached him, Fletcher jumped off and Char leaned back unto his back two legs. The redbird started pounding his feet on the ground. Arden's hands ran up and down his beak while she coaxed him.

"*Wow!* I have not seen him act like that ever! How was camp?"

"Good. It was good," she said.

"How's Aspen? I miss her."

He shrugged his shoulders. "I assume she is great. King Adao has been showing her the ropes. She is interning with him on a legal matter so there is not much time for me to see her. Of course when I do see her, she just preaches about the Sky Laws. King Adao not only takes up my girlfriend's time, but also my dad's. It is annoying. Anyway, I am happy for her."

Arden empathized with him and patted him on the shoulder. "The Kress family is not your typical family, I guess. Sorry." Arden attached her bags to a saddle parcel on Char.

"Well, you ready to go home?" Fletcher walked around Char and helped Arden up. Fletcher jumped on the redbird and together they headed up to their big home in The Sky.

Chapter 17

A STORM WAS coming in and the breeze was strong this morning. Before departing, Fletcher made Arden promise that she would meet him at The University's library later that evening. When Arden asked why, he simply said, "Because…well, you'll see."

These combat boots were getting heavier and heavier as she walked some distance to the front door. Inside the grand entrance, she set her bags down on the floor. The scent of home comforted her, she inhaled in bliss for a moment. She went to the kitchen area where most of the family would congregate throughout the day. As she walked in, she heard voices in the library. She stopped and listened outside the door. It was King Adao and a male having a discussion, something about a promotion and a raise for being a great warrior ("honesty is always the best policy"). Arden continued into the kitchen area. She sat down at the dinner table and ate some fruits that were always displayed there.

Aspen had walked in with a glass of wine in her hand. She chugged the last bit of it and set it down on the table loudly. Her eyes grew large when they finally settled on her little sister. "Arden! I missed you!" her older sister yelled.

They settled down at the table to chat. Loki came in the kitchen and Aspen ordered her to make Arden's coming-home feast. There was a steely edge to Aspen's voice that Loki walked out the room with her tail between her legs to start up the oven.

Arden spoke up. "That was uncalled for. I wanted to see her."

Aspen was taken aback by Arden's honesty. "Well, if that cook means more to you than your own sister, then please go join her."

"What is the matter?" Arden asked, eyeing the empty wine glass.

"Nothing is wrong."

Arden heard whimpering at her feet. She looked down to see Solar. He looked like he had grown some. Arden grabbed him up and gave him kisses on his head. "So, did Ross bring you back, huh, little guy?" As she put Solar on the ground, it hit her. *Why would Solar be in her house?*

At that moment, she heard someone clearing their throat. She looked up and saw King Adao and Ross standing together. King Adao placed his hand on Ross' shoulder and said, "Arden, I just promoted Ross here. He told me of your travels and newfound romance. He has asked for my permission and so I shall give it. Yes, he may have your hand in marriage."

Arden thought she may pass out. She stood up to stand next to Ross and yanked him toward the far side of the room. "Just a moment," she announced to Adao. "What are you doing? I will not go along with this," she whispered.

Ross had his back to the others and looked Arden in the eye. "You will go along with it because I can tell King Adao a lot. I'm sure he would love to hear about Mythias and where he can find him. I'm sure he would want to find him once he heard about your late nights together." Arden's mouth dropped open in disgust. "Look, do this one thing for me. It's not like you can marry him anyway, Arden. It's the least you can do after leading me on like you did. Come on, my job means everything to me."

Arden nodded her head. Perhaps she was about to overreact. Perhaps she should have thought this through more, but the threat was real. She decided she will not have it. Instead, she decided to rip him apart in front of a surprised audience. King Adao, Aspen, and Scyth froze in puzzlement as Arden explained that Ross was a liar and just wanted to advance in his career. Disappointment lingered in the air. Arden took it a step further when she dramatically displayed her scars that Ross gave her. Ross was immediately dragged away for questioning.

King Adao came closer to view and feel the scars himself. Anger flashed in his eyes. "Scyth, you are to take Ross to the special room. We will interrogate him until we get the full story." Arden especially cringed when he yelled next, "Get the nummers ready!" King Adao walked briskly up to Ross, grabbed his face, and spat, "Tit for tat. You too shall be scarred."

Arden immediately regretted this. She did not want them to hurt Ross as much as she was disappointed in him. This left Arden standing in the middle of the room, breathless and vulnerable. The silence was deafening as her elder sister walked away from her and disappeared out the door. Aspen clearly did not support Arden at this moment. Arden yelled King Adao's name out loud.

He came running back into the room and looked confused. "What? What has happened now?"

"Must you use the nummers? Just suspend him."

King Adao's face went eerily flat. He stepped up to Arden and said one sentence that made her shiver. "His pain is now my delight." With his chin lifted high, he marched out the door, leaving Arden in shambles.

The only thing that took precedence to Ross being burnt was that he will tell Adao the truth about Mythias and The Hard Road. This was not the way she wanted King Adao to find out. They were meant to have that crucial conversation while sitting down over a drink, just uncle to niece. Her only hope of having an understanding uncle evaporated due to her unplanned tantrum. She truly hoped that Mythias would not pay for her ignorance. Her stomach churned at the thought of him being inconvenienced by this. Myth tried so hard to go unnoticed and take the easy road. He was right. Arden was a hard road, and she just made it worse. She realized that she needed to get a message to Myth as soon as possible. He needs to get out of harm's way!

Staring at herself in her bedroom mirror, she remembered that Fletcher wanted to meet with her at the library. She needed to give him the message for Myth. Throwing the old clothes out of the bag, she packed it with fresh clean outfits and took off in a hurry. Before leaving the estate, she messaged her friend Fletcher to meet her early at library in ten minutes. She ran outside where a big storm was brewing overhead and one back at her estate, regrettably.

*****

Meanwhile on Earth…

Myth sat with his friend Wick in the empty bar. Wick immediately come over as soon as he heard that Myth was back from camp. His Irish pal was the one who helped push him to visit Arden. Wick took a bite of his tomato-and-ham sandwich. With his mouth full, he muttered, "Have I ever steered you wrong, lad?" His Irish accent still thick even with a full mouth. He grabbed his cold beer and guzzled it down. Myth threw a napkin at his ill-mannered friend who still had mustard on his upper lip. "It'll all be grand. Give her a week. She needs the time, *aye*? Her being royalty and all is going to be hard to sneak, ya know, but that gal will find a way."

"She is a pure one. She's like an angel, but a very sneaky one."

They snickered, thinking back on Arden's gumption and her deep-rooted need to know things. "I'm happy for you and will help you both in any way I can, you know that. If you need hide out somewhere, then I will watch The Hard Road for you. Or if you need to stay at my house, it is all yours. Whatever you need." They both downed another gulp of beer and sat in silence for a moment. Wick asked if Tess ever warmed up to Arden and was surprised when he was told that they became close. "Isn't that a little odd? Your ex with your future one?"

Myth's face became serious and cold. "It's a little odd. My past and my future coming together…but whatever. They are complete opposites but are welcome to be friends." Myth kicked his chair back and planted his feet up on the table. He started to look more relaxed, this was the effect Wick had on him.

"You hear about Dundee?" Wick dared to ask.

Myth placed his feet quickly back on the ground to brace himself. He was silent for moment. "No." He barely spoke the word but had a feeling where this was going. No conversation ever started well when asked that damn question.

"Well, I hate to be the one to tell you and I don't want to bring you down, but he was snatched."

Myth punched the table, rattling the dishes. "When, *goddamnit*? When?"

Wick regretted mentioning it now. "Yesterday. Nothing you can do. Nothing any of us can do."

Myth stood up as anger filled his body. He kicked a chair across the room, causing it to break. "What did he do?"

Placing the dishes on another table out of harm's way, Wick answered, "Dundee. Well, you know he had a big mouth. He did not like being followed so he mouthed off. Called the guy a 'flyfucker' or something like that. I don't know. This Sky Walker wasted no time. He snatched him in the blink of an eye. I think he was just done with it all, ya know. Walking on eggshells is no way to live."

Dundee was part of the secret army Myth helped create. He was the fun and wild one who just wanted to blow stuff up, the one to crack jokes and make light of everything, the one who did not let things get to him. He was strong. Now he is dead. Myth took a deep breath to calm himself down. He grabbed his chair and plopped down on it. "It is an everyday thing these days. We decided a while ago that we no longer fight, but we will also no longer run. We stand and protect our family. We do not initiate and we do not bring attention to ourselves…Dundee wasn't good at that." Myth exhaled loudly and looked back at his wall. "We Don't Run!" was written boldly, it was their mantra. He closed his eyes for a moment to try to hold on to his sanity.

"He will be remembered fondly. To Dundee!"

They rose their glasses up high and clinked them together while yelling a manly "aye."

"Let's get drunk and devise a plan to take down King Adao for once and for all!" Myth roared loudly.

*****

Arden ran down the dark street while her packed bag bobbed back and forth behind her. She was on a mission to meet Fletcher. She thought back on what he had said earlier today. "Because I know you will want to talk to someone later. You'll see."

She wondered how he knew and why he did not tip her off so she would not be surprised. Irked, she turned down a street corner and strolled through the entrance of The University, rather briskly. Her hair and bright feathers flew back as she looked down both directions. Making her way to the library, she yelled Fletcher's name to see if he was already there. The library was as glorious as L. Ward's Library on Earth but was much bigger and looked like a grand cathedral. The rain started to pour harder, hitting the stained-glass windows on the exterior walls with such force that shattering the glass was a possibility. Walking over to a huge dark marble table, she stood by it while surveying her surroundings. No one was here. She flipped her domed bracelet up and saw that Fletcher had left her another message.

"Arden, I will be there. But I have a small task to complete before coming up to The Sky. I'll be there in about twenty minutes."

Frustrated, she quickly recorded her message to send back to him. "Make it quick, Mr. Fletcher Haderbee. This is *urgent*!"

She felt the panic rush through her body down to her toes. Ross was getting closer and closer to revealing her love for a human who will be hunted down and killed for all she knows. She will not let this happen. Somehow, someway she will control this situation, she tried to convince herself.

*****

Back on Earth…

Wick laughed aloud at Mythias. He thought he was kidding about devising a plan to take down Adao. Myth's straight face and anger was apparent that his intentions were as real as the situation they were in.

"Holy hell! No! Do not even think about it. You know what happened when you dabbled in this before. Your brother ended up dying. It is a death sentence to fight against these beings. Open your eyes, mate! Focus on the light and not the dark." Wick stood up and backed away from him. He knew that look. He knew his friend very well. There was no changing his mind when he looked like that.

"I'm doing this with or without you. I've been teetering for a long while on this. I can't stand by and have another friend die for nothing. I will not. And if it was you instead of Dundee, I think you'd have a different outlook on this too, Wick." Myth jumped up in a haste and sprinted down to his bedroom at the back of the house. He grabbed an army bag and placed it on his bed as he went through his belongings. He will need some clothes, tools, and food on his journey. He grabbed some clothes from his closet, personal hygiene products, a few badges, and an army jacket. Storming back up to the bar area, he saw Wick about to leave. He had his hand on the doorknob.

"Go ahead and go. I'm leaving anyway." Myth grabbed some drinks from the bar area, beef jerky, and medicine and then threw them in his bag for safekeeping. "Where you going, exactly?" Wick asked, worried.

Myth walked to the door to join him. "I'm going to find all my army brothers. I'm going to recruit, but this time, I will win or die trying. This is a hard road but I'm taking it. I wish you would too, my friend."

Wick stood there with a smile on his face. He brushed his hand through his shaggy hair and laughed. "I'm coming. I've been waiting on you to gather your shit. Let's get going, Runner Boy."

"Yep, let's go do this." After locking up the bar, they were at the beginning of a journey to freedom, and it felt astounding. They shuffled down the road and past the big warrior post. Myth recognized Fletcher from afar jogging to a phoenix. "He looks like he's in a hurry," he said aloud then Myth yelled, "HEY, FLETCHER!"

Fletcher had jumped on his phoenix and was in full stride when he heard his name. He turned his head around and stopped the bird. Marching quickly back his way, Fletcher seemed rushed and frustrated for the interruption. "I gotta go! Arden has sent for me and it is urgent. What do you need?" he asked quickly.

"Urgent? Well, when you see her, tell her that I'm going to be gone for a week or so. I will explain everything to her when I see her next. Tell her not to worry about me."

Fletcher nodded his head and did not say anything. He was on his own type of journey as he turned around and sped away on his firebird. Myth and Wick stood there for a moment and watched as he galloped into the distance.

"Don't you think this is something you should discuss with Arden first? She may not appreciate you killing her uncle, after all."

Myth became deathly silent, kicked the dirt, and continued to tread with a purpose.

*****

She found herself tapping her oversized combat boot in impatience. "Where are you?" she asked no one in particular.

Even though she was eager to see Fletcher, she could not deny the beauty around her. The aisles of books were just screaming her name. She wanted to devour them all, to grab an armful and sneak back to a comfortable corner to escape this world. She wished to go back to simpler times, but nothing was going to be the simple ever again. Her views, feelings, wisdom, and soul had evolved. You cannot go back to what you were no matter how hard you try. A deflowered virgin will never be innocent again. You cannot force a freed genie back in his bottle. Ultimately, you cannot encourage a sky girl to go back to being blind and ignorant. She was caught up in one issue after another, one beautiful disaster after another. All issues stemmed around her uncle and his disapproval for things.

Bending over to massage her toes, she needed to stretch and breathe deeply. Right there in the oversized library, she prayed to God and asked that he give her strength to get through this and a positive outcome. Mid-stretch, she heard footsteps pounding the glossy floor beneath her. She found herself holding her breath in anticipation. Finally, Fletcher came hustling in with a bag on his back, his face still painted as a Scout.

"My goodness! You nearly scared me to death," she complained.

He grabbed a cloth from his bag and wiped his face roughly until it was all gone. He swung the bag off his back and laid it on the marble table. When he was done, he turned to her and said, "I've got a lot of news. What do you want to hear first? The really bad news or not-so-bad news?"

Arden answered, "No, *I* have news and I need you to listen to me first. I have a message for Myth that you need to give him as soon as possible!"

He shook his head. All of a sudden, a tear ran down his face. He grabbed a seat and held his head in his paint-stained hands. "Why does it have to be me?"

This stopped Arden in her tracks. *Why was this a competition for who had the bigger of news?* Offering a hand on his shoulder, she tapped him and kneeled to the ground to make eye contact. "You are scaring me, Fletcher. Why are you so upset?" Arden's face softened. She wanted to take care of him.

"Take a deep breath. No matter what news you have for me…it will be fine. You will be fine. I will be fine. We will get through it. It will all be okay." He straightened his spine back out and stared at her. She had never seen such a look on a Sky Walker's face before.

"Want to tell me the not-so-bad news first?" she asked softly. Arden felt like she was speaking to an injured animal or child, not a warrior of The Sky.

He shook his head up and down. "Myth…I bumped into Myth on the way here. He wanted me to tell you that he will be gone for a few weeks and not to worry about him."

She exhaled loudly with relief. "Thank goodness! I needed him to get away from The Hard Road! You can dismiss my message now. That takes care of it. By the way, did you know about Ross' plans?"

"Yes, I knew. I wanted you to be surprised. I heard about Myth putting you through the wringer. Ross told me everything. How close you two had become and that he was going to confess his love for you, but he needed King Adao's approval first." Arden proceeded to tell him all about Ross and the issues he caused her. It all began to make sense for Fletcher. He could see now why she was in such a hurry. King Adao will be hunting Myth down by sundown. "Luckily, Myth will be gone for a while. I will check his place when he gets back. I'll let him know everything." He was starting to sound more and more like himself.

Arden smiled, relieved. She took another breath to steady herself. "So do I dare ask about the bad news?"

Fletcher walked over to his bag and came back with a folded-up paper in his hand. He swallowed hard and looked Arden in the eye. "Remember when I told you that I had a task to complete before I'd meet you?" She nodded. "Well, Professor Greiner and Bianca needed me. I rushed over to them at the camp and was handed this newspaper and told a story. I'm told you recruited them to investigate King Adao and a love affair." He looked at her expectantly.

She realized where he was going with this. She became excited to hear all about it. She could use this information when she spoke to Adao next. Relief started to come over her as she stepped closer to him.

"Let me explain something before you look at this newspaper. Turns out, King Adao visited Earth quite frequently without the knowledge of King Oswin. He was studying the humans and their culture. Adao felt they were greedy and needed guidance. Anyway, he would wear a bandana over his face to hide his sharp nose and wear dark human clothes to blend in as much as possible during his research. One day, he noticed this human and became very interested in her. He would fly down just to watch her. He eventually tried romancing the writer. Long story short, she had taken a liking to him. Like turned to love even when he showed her his true form one day. When their relationship became turbulent, she threatened to write a story about his people and expose him for the fraud he was. They bickered and argued. She tested him by writing make-believe stories of the "Man of the Sky" that turned out to be all true. She wrote stories daily. The humans loved it, they ate it up. She became well-known because of her articles. He was angered by her stories and threatened her to stop. He said he would have her killed if she continued, but she kept publishing story after story to spite him. He would visit her day after day and tell her to stop, but he was head over heels for this woman that they were just empty threats. She finally broke it off with him when she found out about something horrible he had done. I have the last article she had written in my hand. She was banished from her people, mostly to keep her safe and out of Adao's reach. Arden, just read it. I'm so sorry."

Arden carefully grabbed the old newspaper out of his hand and stopped for a second. *What could be so bad? What could cause Fletcher to shed a tear? What had Adao done?* She sighed and said, "Here goes nothing." She opened the newspaper and held it in front of her as she stood in the middle of the library. She noticed the headline, which read in big black font, "Family from The Sky Murdered!" Her breath hitched. She had an odd feeling she was getting a glimpse into her past. Such a sad day for her and her people. She looked up at Fletcher. "Thanks for the paper. At least I'll know more…"

Her words trailed off when she saw a large picture with great details of the attack under the headline. The picture was of her beloved mother holding her little brother in her arms tightly while running away from the attack. Her father, King Oswin, was hunched over in pain as a human attacked him with a large knife. Everything stopped. She lost the ability to draw breath. Standing like a statue, she finally lifted her eyes up to Fletcher in blatant shock. Her beautiful almond eyes were in complete disbelief. Like a fish with no water, she was barely standing, threatening to faint from the revelation. The human who attacked her family was a man with a bandana around his face and dressed in all black. A man she calls her uncle. King Adao killed her family when he was posing as a human.

*****

Myth had met with three of his army friends so far. To no surprise, they all were on board and told him to sign them all up. Myth did use Dundee as the fuel to ignite their hate, but they deserved to know and he needed them on his side. He had better odds with more men in his secret army. It was starting to get late so he and Wick stayed the night at Ben's house. Ben let them stay in a bunkhouse on the property where they started drawing out maps and plans. He used his memory to draw out weapons they could make with scrap metals. Myth knew all this was going to take some time but it would all be worth it. He had nothing but time on his hands. The three of them sat around a card table, sketching their own ideas. They discussed the route to each house that Myth's army friends lived at. They would hit each house and recruit while he would go out and recruit more people. This secret army will not be so secret when he was done with it. Myth was on a mission.

*****

Arden fell down to her knees while salty tears gushed from her eyes as severe as the rainstorm outside. Thunder and lightning bombarded the place, making everything shake. Arden did not notice. She was in a hellish emotional place she could not comprehend at all. Fletcher was bent down next to her, trying to console her, but she could not hear his words. She could not feel his touch. She was going through an internal transformation. When she finally found her voice, she screamed in anguish, "NOOOOOO!" She hit the ground with her hand, her talons cutting her palm. Still sobbing, she was consumed with fire inside, getting brighter and brighter and hotter and hotter. She wiped away her tears in a slow fashion and noticed an ashy substance smeared along with the tears in her eyes. She did not understand why ash was coming from her eyes.

Her uncle had killed her family so he could rule the kingdom and take over the humans that he had been researching illegally. *How dare he call her daughter! How dare he call her family!* She began to pant heavily as the fire within was starting to consume her.

Fletcher grabbed her and helped stand her up on her feet. His words were starting to come in clearer as she tried to ignore the ashy burn in her eyes. "Arden, listen to me. Aspen knew this whole time! She found out years ago. We must talk to her and get more answers. I think my girlfriend is in love with King Adao."

Chapter 18

SOME MINUTES PASSED. Arden finally cleared her head. She found her voice and said, "Not possible, Fletcher. Aspen would never hide this. You got the wrong information!"

Fletcher grabbed her hurt hand and held it gently. "Yes, she does know. I am certain of it. Look, I have messaged her to meet me here. I want answers, I am sure you do too." Fletcher walked to the table with his heart broken. "I can't believe I've been following his Sky Laws this whole time. He's a fraud."

Arden had not moved, transfixed at a very large crystal mirror across the room. Staring back at her was a female Sky Walker with black ash caked around her almond eyes. It was heavy and smoky. She tried picking it off her face but it would not budge. She had not seen anyone cry ashes before. *It can't be a good sign*, she thought. It did, however, look mystically beautiful as if she was a wearing a black mask. She stumbled away, still reeling over all the information that came to light. She needed more answers. She felt different inside as if something had been awakened.

Aspen came rushing in from the right side of the library. Arden's head snapped in her sister's direction. Beat

Fletcher to the punch, she asked, "Did you know? Did you know about Adao killing our family? Tell me now!" She demanded with a clear voice of authority, a threatening tone she has never used before in her life. Arden turned Aspen around her to face her. Fletcher tried to step in front of Arden but she pushed him to the side as if he weighed nothing. "ANSWERS…NOW!"

Aspen flinched as if the words smacked her now flushed face. She then lifted her head high and muttered a simple yes. Arden's head tilted to the side in comprehension. Aspen began talking quickly, "I can explain. I found out when I was a little girl. I was spying on Adao and Scyth a few days after the funeral. Adao and Scyth, dressed as humans, attacked and killed them."

Arden spoke deliberately. "I want you to take me back to the day *my* family was murdered by this man you protect. *My* family! They no longer count as yours."

Aspen swallowed and began her story. "There was a human lady he was in love with, I guess. A writer down on Earth who he thought was brilliant. He said she was filled with fire much like a phoenix. He would peek in her window and watch her write in her living room. He said that he finally had the nerve to bump into her. I guess the relationship started soon after. He was in love. *Oh*, Arden! He made love sound so…so otherworldly." Arden's expression hardened. "Anyway, I gathered that he had been doing some major planning with Scyth because one of them said it took them months to get the plan rolling, trying to schedule the first visit on Earth for our family perfectly. Adao had the idea for Father to take Sawyer and Mother because it would make him appear less threatening. A man from The Sky alone could be seen as a threat, but a male with his loving family by his side would appeal to people long enough to hear that they come in peace. Obviously, the plan worked. Father did as what was suggested by Adao. Scyth was a big part of this. I heard something about how he did many of behind-the-scenes-type tasks. For example, he placed an order on the warriors that they stick to The Sky, that no one be on foot near our family. That is why no one was close by to interfere with Adao and protect our family. The attack was super quick. Scyth protected Adao and they quickly ran into the writer's house. I heard she was angry when she found out what they had done. She didn't like that the humans were going to be blamed for such a monstrosity."

Arden put her hand up for Aspen to hold on for a moment. "Just to clarify, no humans were involved in the attack? It was just Adao? He's responsible for this war with the humans?" Heat was radiating off Arden's body as she spoke.

"That is right," Aspen's voice was light and fragile as she continued, "It caused an uproar amongst the humans. They panicked and started running to their homes."

Arden had heard enough about what happened that tragic day. A day that her sister knew about for many, many years but stood by Adao and kept his dirty little secret. Aspen became tearful as Arden stared her down like a wolf to a lamb.

"I had to forgive him. He was our only family, Arden. He was everything. Then he became our king. I wanted to tell you but I knew you would hate him so I kept it a secret." She stepped back some and looked down. "I was a scared little girl who found comfort in him. No matter his reason, I have forgiven him. He created the new Sky Laws. I believe in those words. I believe in his justice and principles. I preach those sacred words every single day of my life. It is all I know. He's not a bad person, though you may hate him."

Fletcher stepped in. "My father is just as guilty." He stood there shaking his head and looking confused. He then remembered a certain question that he had been dying to ask her. "I heard that you love him. So…do you?"

Aspen looked down at her cold bare feet. "Yes."

"Family love or love *love*?"

Arden watched Aspen's face and knew the answer before she even uttered a word. Aspen hesitated for a moment. "I love *love* him. And…well, Fletcher, he wants to marry me. I want to be married to him more than anything in this world but it would be viewed as an abomination by our people. I don't know how this will work out…"

Arden started to feel that furious fire deep down inside her rise up the surface, engulfing her. The feeling of smoke filled her desperate lungs, she could hardly breathe. Arden's thoughts were flying through her dangerous mind. *No wonder this man looked at Aspen as an equal and me like a child! That is why he would call me "daughter" and not her. No wonder he favored Aspen all these years! She was with her uncle.* Too much wrongdoing. Too much betrayal. Arden screamed, "*Aaah!*" She began to pant heavily as black ashes started to form and slowly rise from her hands. A small black tornado swirled in front of her, blowing her hair in the air. In an instant, her scarred hand grew larger as did her black-painted talons.

Her spine went *crack!* She doubled over in pain. Next, black-colored foam came spewing out of her mouth that shortly became smoky clouds midair. Deep noises issued from her throat, causing Aspen and Fletcher to jump back. A deep growling noise. They were staring in disbelief as her petite body writhed repeatedly. Forward and back. Forward and back again. Her bony left shoulder popped out of place, extending nearly to her left earlobe while her right arm elongated down closer to her knee. She hunched over for a moment in dead silence. Ash swirled through the air and floated toward the floor. Fletcher and Aspen eyed each other. There were no words spoken.

*****

Myth tried hitting his flat pillow many times, hoping it would give his head some support during his sleep tonight. The pillow and sheets were nice and cold against his overheated skin. Just talking about these plans excited him. *Revenge will be his*, he thought.

He rolled over and stared at the dull gray ceiling above him. In his white shirt and boxers, he laid there thinking a million things. When it was all said and done, it was not the revenge that consumed most of his thoughts, it was Arden. Sweet Arden. He tucked his hands behind his head and smiled. He thought back on the first time he saw her. He noticed her walking by, completely out of place. He observed her laughing with her friends and drinking that honey mead for the first time from a dark corner. He could not help it. He laughed to himself and blushed. He had never seen someone so lovely and attractive in his life. He knew she was something very special. Glimpses of Arden's perfect face flashed through his mind. He closed his eyes, letting his thoughts run wild. Thinking of their arguments, fixing breakfast together, having deep talks, kissing in his bed, caring for her wounds, and walking together. And he will never forget that that one glorious night under the stars. He thought about the way her hair smelled, the curve of her back, and her gentleness. She was everything he needed.

He took a huge breath and rolled over on his side. He would never be able to sleep tonight at this rate.

*****

They were too fearful to move an inch. Minutes passed. Finally, Aspen took a small step forward and said Arden's name aloud. She inched closer to her and lightly touched her back. "Please, Arden!" Her voice trembled with deep concern. Aspen got a good look at the scars on Arden's neck and was disgusted.

WOOSH! Arden leaped up instantly, showing her altered form. Her bright eyes changed to a deep golden yellow, a stark contrast to the onyx-colored ash that surrounded her eyes. Her nose had grown more into the shape of a beak. Arden was not Arden. This unpredictable, powerful, dark being appeared right before their eyes! She moved slowly and menacingly toward Aspen, looking her dead in the eye. Arden was more birdlike than ever. Swiftly, Arden tipped her head back where her chin was to The Sky. Then opened her mouth, wider than humanly possible, and let out a large growl followed by fiercely hot, bright blue fire. She breathed fire directly on her sister, stepping back to watch her burn. Aspen screamed in pain as the fire burned her entire body. Arden spit on her wailing sister as an afterthought.

Fletcher stood with his mouth open, frozen in fear. He did not know what to do. He just saw the love of his life burned alive. Fight Arden or help Aspen? Aspen ran out of the room blazing and screaming at the top of her lungs. Fletcher could not move.

"Stop, drop, and roll Sis," Arden spat under her breath.

Fletcher stared at her—or whatever this being now was—and waited to make his move.

*****

Myth could not sleep with all this reminiscing filling his head. He sat up and tried to think what was bothering him. He massaged the space between his eyes. He had been against taking the hard roads in life yet he continued to choose them. Hard road one, Arden. Hard road two, secret army. Hard road three, leaving his bar. That bar meant a lot to him. It was a steady income and shelter from this crazy world. It protected him. It made him connect to others when he was deep down a shy person. To think of possibly giving it up made him nervous. Did he really want to rattle the cage when he was currently somewhat comfortable? In addition, would Arden be upset with him for all of this? Bringing people together to attack her uncle could possibly make him lose her. Is this secret army worth the loss of the bar and her? The possible loss of his life? He did not want to answer those questions.

"Can't sleep?" Wick was lying down on a cot next to him. He rolled over to look at Mythias. "You having second thoughts?"

Myth had too many questions in head, let alone Wick throwing some at him. "I don't know, man. Got a lot on my mind. I don't want to make the wrong decision. It's one of the biggest decisions of my life."

Wick shook his head in agreement. He recognized the weight of all this but he knew he and Myth would pull through. "You'll make the right decision. I think you're making it now, honestly. King Adao needs someone to show him that we are just as important as him and his people. That we are strong and we used to have freedom. We will have freedom once more, lad. I can feel it. The New United States of America."

Myth laughed at his optimism. "Coming from the man who didn't want to join me a few hours ago."

Wick flipped him off and chuckled. "May I ask you a serious question?" Wick asked with a smile. Myth grabbed his boot and threw it at him. They cackled into the night and teased one another. "In all seriousness, I have to ask you something."

Myth rolled his eyes and responded with "Well, spit it out, if you must." Then a few moments passed in silence. "*Wow!* This must be a serious question."

Wick sat up and placed his feet on the ground. "Say I survive all this, would you mind horribly if I hung out with Tess some?"

Myth's eyes opened wide. He was not expecting that and, quite honestly, they were polar opposites. "You think you can handle pure evil?"

They howled with more laughter as Wick picked the boot up and threw it back at Myth.

*****

Back at The Sky…

"Fletcher, do not go after her. She got what she deserved."

The command was real, even her voice sounded different. Menacing. Arden strolled over to the bright blue fire still burning on the floor. "I would never hurt you. I will kill only those who betray me. I know what you are thinking." She walked over to him cautiously. "Yes, I am Arden. Just a different *version* of me. I will explain everything later. But for now, I have a king to dethrone and bury."

She pulled her long blue-and-gold robe over her head, revealing her half naked body, wearing only white underwear and muddy combat boots. Then she tossed the clothes into the hungry fire. This version of Arden did not care that her bare chest was exposed to the world. Secondly, she did not want to be a Sky Walker any longer. She would stand with the humans now and forever. They were her home and she will protect them. Quickly extending her right hand back with all her strength, she pulled her gorgeous blue feathers out of her aching head. A yelp escaped her lips. She thought she had all three but only one was left intact. She looked at the bloody blue feathers and threw them into the fire next. Everything went into slow motion after that.

Fletcher decided to join her on her way out of the burning library. As she ran down The University halls, she blew fire and ash from her mouth causing more disaster. She is going to burn everything that honored Adao. They dashed outside into the drizzling rain. The dark thunderstorm above was violent, but this did not deter Arden and her gift for fire. She pushed through and started to throw blue fire from the palm of her hand at all the different places that King Adao frequently visited. Everything he loved will burn down to the ground. Everything that was built on lies and deceit would be no more. Her people deserved to know the truth. They will learn it in time. Floating her way into the dark, wet streets, a full-grown Solar came running up to her. Fletcher could not believe his eyes. Was he living in a different world where nothing made sense anymore?

She bent down to greet her friend and said, "About time, Octavius." Fletcher decided to bite his tongue and went with it.

The three of them made their way through as if in slow motion again. Arden was causing the land in The Sky to burn brightly razing The Sky to the ground. People were looking out their windows in bewilderment, trying to make sense of such a sight. This was not something they see every day in utopia. They made their way up a grassy hill to where they could see her huge home in the distance. It stood large and seemed indestructible. She knew that at any time, the warriors would be on her tail and she would welcome them. The wind was strong and blew some of her long hair away from her hair clip. She stood proudly on top the hill with blood dripping down her neck onto her one prominent blue feather. Bare-chested and with her talons in full extension, she was ready to fight the fight. Fletcher and Octavius stood behind her, also looking out into the distance. She was a threat to Adao's perfect world. She will take him down, no doubt. Revenge for her father, mother, and brother was tangible. She shouted out into the hillside, "I am the legendary blue phoenix! I am Queen Araline reincarnated! And you will burn, my king. The eerily voice sang… "Tit for tat, Adao. You too shall be scarred."

To be continued…

Reference

Song title "Wild Things" sang by Alessia Cara.

About the Author

THE IDEA FOR *Arden of Fire* came to Brooke when she was on an airplane flying home from a mother-daughter vacation in 2016. The original idea was to make it into a comic book but quickly transitioned into the book you are holding today.

Born and raised in Ohio, Brooke dreamt of being a published author from a young age. Her first book was written when she was in the eighth grade but never seen the light of day. Because of her love for writing and Ireland, it was called *The Way to Galway*.

Entering her young adult life, she mainly focused on receiving her bachelor of business administration and created a career in healthcare administration. Brooke was married in 2004 and has three sons.

She is currently working on her second book as a continuation of Arden of Fire. She hopes that readers get immersed in the world that her mind has lovingly lived in for years.

Arden deserves to be known. Better yet,
she deserves to be heard and loved.

—Brooke McCatherine

CPSIA information can be obtained
at www.ICGtesting.com
Printed in the USA
LVHW041750160223
739686LV00003B/225